IRISH ✦ DAYS

IRISH ✳ DAYS

TERRY WOGAN

WITH PHOTOGRAPHS BY MICHAEL J. STEAD

MICHAEL JOSEPH – LONDON

MICHAEL JOSEPH LTD

Published by the Penguin Group
27 Wrights Lane, London W8 5TZ, England
Viking Penguin Inc., 40 West 23rd Street, New York,
New York 10010, USA
Penguin Books Australia Ltd, Ringwood, Victoria,
Australia
Penguin Books Canada Ltd, 2801 John Street, Markham,
Ontario, Canada L3R 1B4
Penguin Books (NZ) Ltd, 182–190 Wairau Road,
Auckland 10, New Zealand

Penguin Books Ltd, Registered Offices: Harmondsworth,
Middlesex, England

First published 1988

Typeset by Goodfellow and Egan, Cambridge
Printed and bound in The Netherlands by Roto Smeets
b.v.

A CIP catalogue record for this book is available from the
British Library

ISBN 0–7181–3248–3

Contents

Acknowledgements

My sincere thanks to Jo Gurnett, who, as usual, did all the *real* work with nary a Grecian bend, nor a cross word.

To John Ranelagh, whose *Ireland: an Illustrated History* taught me more than ten years of swotting in school.

Brian Cleeve, whose *A View of Ireland* was illuminating and instructive.

To Mike, without whose glowing pictures of the land we both love, my words would be as chaff on the wind.

And to Ireland, and its people, without whom it would be just a pretty picture . . . .

And from Mike, a special thank you to Eric Kitching of Kitching Processing Services of Scarborough for his tender loving care of the photographic material.

Prologue

Before you pocket this ravishing work, beguiled by its exquisite photographs and finely-chased finish, a word, dear reader. I have no wish to stumble across you in some dark corner, whimpering over a lack of order, or a dearth of historical fact. This is no guided tour of the Four Green Fields of Ireland, nor indeed, a Plain Man's Guide to Ireland Through the Ages. It's just my view of a land, and a people, that I love. And if it turns out to be more about the people than the land, I can't help you there, either. Like anywhere else, the people make the place. Only in the case of Ireland and the Irish, more so . . . .

Planning and organisation have never been a forte of the Irish and certainly not of this particular Irishman, so if you're coming on this trip, come prepared for a bit of a wander, a meander down the boreens, through the meadows, over the fields, and don't bother with the map. To paraphrase the old Irish story, 'if that's the class of things you were looking for, you shouldn't have started from here in the first place . . . .'

Childhood in Limerick

I started in Limerick, so that's as good a place as any to begin our ramble. The City of the Broken Treaty, where once again, perfidious Albion did the dirty on our brave boys, and sent them across the seas (with a Wogan or two amongst them) to become the Wild Geese, soldiers of fortune in the service of the French, the Austrians or the Stuarts. The hero of the Siege of Limerick by the Williamites in 1691 was one Patrick Sarsfield, who died still fighting William of Orange at the Battle of Landen in Flanders with the words 'would that this were for Ireland!' on his dying lips. They named the bridge over the Shannon after him, and from it, you can see King John's Castle and, nearby, the stone on which the Broken Treaty itself was signed. Ah, but then there's a lot of that in Irish history, and I'd just as soon you didn't start crying into your porter just yet. I know every inch of Sarsfield Bridge; I cycled over it four times a day, back and forward from Crescent College to home, from childhood to boyhood to adolescence. I owe my manly thews, the cause of so much favourable comment, to the cycling trips up hill and down dale. It seems to me, on reflection, that I spent most of my life on a bicycle.

There is a wonderful story by Myles Na Gopaleen in which a policeman, after many years a-wheel, finds himself turning into a bicycle. I'm glad I didn't read it, in the course of a velocipede-ridden childhood, or I might have begun to believe it . . . .

When I wasn't on my own bicycle I was on my father's.

When I was very young, he used to take me on the crossbar of that self-same bicycle and on a Sunday, as a kind of treat, we would travel together, him cycling and me sitting, to that fine purveyor of victuals to the gentry, Leverette and Frye, O'Connell Street, Limerick and I would sit among the raisins and hams while he did the book work. On the way home, he'd stop for a half-pint at Willie 'Bokkles' Gleeson's pub. Willie was called 'Bokkles', because of a small speech deficiency.

You didn't get away with much in Limerick. The merest hint of a squint, and you were known as 'boss-eyed' for the rest of your adolescent life. *Everybody* of my acquaintance had a nickname. There was 'Rogers' (after Roy Rogers, singing cowboy – the man who later had Trigger stuffed. Trigger was his horse. Do I have to explain *everything*?), 'Bonk', 'Flicker', 'Mo', and I was 'Bawky'. Don't ask. I remember clearly when the leader of the gang, 'Rogers', got us all together in solemn conclave, and named us, off the top of his head. He left for Dublin with his family shortly afterwards, leaving his loyal lieutenants to battle on alone with their stigmata. Thanks a lot, Rogers.

POWERSCOURT

This is me pretending I own the place, and that's the Great Sugar Loaf Mountain in the background.

THE GALTEE MOUNTAINS IN CO TIPPERARY

Looking east from the road between Galbally and Ballaghaderg Bridge. The ringing word 'Galtee' has always been associated in my mind with a brand of spreadable cheese. The mountains complement the name; the cheese was pretty good, too . . . .

My father never took more than a half of Guinness with 'Bokkles'. He was an abstemious man, the Da'. He had to be, money was tight all over in the Ireland of the 40s and 50s, and he'd never known it any other way, right from his childhood in 'Ireland's loveliest village', Enniskerry, County Wicklow. My father never talked much about his childhood; he adored his mother and hated his father, flung a slate at his schoolteacher, and left Enniskerry under a cloud to become a grocer's curate in Bray, County Wicklow. Bray is on the coast, about twelve miles from Dublin, ideally situated between two headlands, with a long beach, and perfect for a holiday resort, which it has been for more than a hundred and fifty years. In my youth, it resembled a British holiday place more

SARSFIELD BRIDGE ACROSS THE RIVER SHANNON IN LIMERICK

I know every inch of this blessed bridge having cycled across it four times a day, between home and school, for years.

On the bridge is a memorial to the fourteen leaders who were executed following the 1916 Uprising, and to Tom Clarke in particular; he was a Fenian of the old school and the oldest participant in what was called 'The Poets' Rebellion'.

than an Irish one, with slot-machine arcades and fun fairs along its promenade. Indeed, right up to the 60s, Bray attracted the kind of British holiday-maker that you'd think more likely in Blackpool, Great Yarmouth or the Isle of Man. Not many of their ilk patronise the place these days (well Benidorm's cheaper, even if you can't get a nice cuppa tea) but there's still an indefinable whiff of West Britain off Bray. Just as there is about Greystones, further down the coast of Wicklow. As with a number of small towns in Ireland, these pretty seaside places have an ambience that seems more British than Irish. Or maybe it's just me. My mother says I always *was* a sensitive child . . . .

The Da hated Bray, probably because he spent the best years of his life there, humping tea-chests and packing sugar into brown bags, before crawling exhausted to his attic, above the store. Although I loved to visit his old home in Enniskerry and meet my cousins, my father wasn't all that keen on returning there either. Painful childhood memories had something to do with it, and he couldn't walk down the street without reminding himself of having to step off the pavement into the road to make way for his betters, who seemed to include everybody from the school teacher to Lord Powerscourt. Enniskerry was part of the Powerscourt Demesne, and Powerscourt House still

Enniskerry, Co Wicklow

The Powerscourt Arms Hotel confirms the close connection the town had with the Powerscourt Demesne. Enniskerry was once considered to be the prettiest village in Ireland but a recent visit showed there to have been many changes. However, I spent a most convivial hour in this hostelry (see illustration on page 94) and they remembered the family name. I was also glad to see that my cousin's shop still stands just off the main street.

Wicklow

OVERLEAF Wicklow is a pretty seaside town on the east coast of Ireland, and the sandy beaches look over a wide bay. It's called 'Wickla' by the locals. While we're at it, Carlow is also called 'Carla'. Tullow, however, where the wife's people live, is called 'Tullow' because there's another place called 'Tulla'. It's got a famous Ceili band, but that need not detain us here . . . .

POWERSCOURT

Powerscourt House still dominates the beautiful Wicklow landscape. Its vast garden is considered to be one of the most outstanding in Europe.

THE RUINED ABBEY AT HILL OF SLANE, CO MEATH

dominates the beautiful Wicklow landscape, even if the Powerscourts themselves are long gone. Powerscourt is now a gutted ruin of a great Georgian House with a magnificent view over formal gardens. You'll see the ruins of many more as you wander around, or perhaps as you meander up the Shannon. Great, empty, decaying shells of houses, with their neglected yew walks, and long since overgrown gardens. Many were put to the torch, in a welter of misguided Republican fervour, during the Irish Civil War of the early 20s.

The Wogans had their great houses, too, just in case you think you're dealing with rubbish here. Clongowes, Wood Castle, an imposing site that sits atop a hill overlooking the plains of Royal Meath, was one of our ancestral seats. It's now a Jesuit school. Malahide Castle, overlooking Dublin Bay, was another Wogan *pied-à-terre*. Now it's a hotel. I can't tell you how, or where, we slipped up and lost the old homesteads. We probably acquired them in the time-honoured way, by knocking the sitting tenant over the head.

Two examples of the empty decaying shells of Ireland's once-great houses: RIGHT *Roonaun, a fortified house of early vintage, near Meelick, Co Tipperary;* ABOVE *and a house in the Anglo-Irish style near Bruff, Co Limerick.*

THE WICKLOW HILLS

Near Sally Gap and Glencree. The landscape of these hills can at one moment remind you of the English Chilterns and the next of the North York Moors.

The Wogans in Ireland

The Wogans crossed the Irish Sea with the first wave of Norman predators, in the twelfth century, from Anglesey in North Wales. Indeed, the name 'Wogan' is still more to be seen in Wales than in Ireland. It derives from the Welsh 'Gwgan' which means 'glum'. But you hardly needed me to tell you that! Anyway, somewhere in the twelfth century our gang nipped across with as big a crowd of louts, hooligans, soldiers of fortune as poor old Ireland hadn't seen since the Norman's ancestors, the Vikings, some four centuries previously.

THE RUINED CHURCH AT HILL OF SLANE, CO MEATH

THE 13TH-CENTURY COLLEGIATE CHURCH AT KILMALLOCK, CO LIMERICK

Killala, Co Mayo

The round tower is 84 feet high and rises up out of the pretty town.

Like their ancestors, the Normans liked what they saw and took it . . . . They came, saw and conquered, through the usual mixture of tribal treachery and jealousy and with the approval of the Pope, Adrian IV. Mind you, he was the only *English* pope in history. In 1155, he granted the lordship of Ireland to King Henry II of England, so that 'he might bring the trust of the Christian faith to the ignorant and rude Irish'. This was particularly rich coming from the Pope, in view of the fact that it was Ireland, its monks, artists and scholars, that had single-handedly kept the Christian faith, as well as art and literature, going during the Dark Ages that had enveloped Europe since the Fall of Rome in the fifth century.

In 600AD there had been more than eight hundred monasteries in Ireland. It was the only bastion of Christianity against the barbarians, keeping the flame of Christianity alight in a dark Europe. From all these monasteries, hundreds of missionaries and monks went to keep the flame of the Gospel and the Christian faith alive throughout the rest of Europe. The remains of these monasteries can be seen all along the Shannon, in Birr and Clonfert for example, but particularly Clonmacnoise. The monastery at Clonmacnoise was founded in 548 by St Ciaran. The great St Colmcille founded monasteries in Derry, Durrow and Kells before he sailed to Iona, on the west coast of Scotland, where he founded one of the great Christian schools. It was the monks of Iona, it is said, that kept

CLONMACNOISE IN CO OFFALY

Clonmacnoise was founded in the 6th century, and through-out its history – until it was finally abandoned in 1552 – it is said to have faced numerous attacks by Viking raiders and medieval English armies, and even its own Irish neighbours didn't leave it alone, battering it consistently.

ABOVE *O'Rourke's Tower, Clonmacnoise and* RIGHT *some of the superb crosses with the ruins of the medieval church behind.*

GLENDALOUGH, CO WICKLOW

This magnificent round tower is 103 feet high.

and maintained the Christian faith in England and Scotland through the dark centuries. It was in those years that Ireland became known as the Island of Saints and Scholars; not just Irish scholars, but scholars who were there to escape from the barbarian hordes who were burning and plundering most of Europe. In the tenth and eleventh centuries, the monks took to building round towers; you can see many relics of the round towers to this day in Ireland – with a window half way up. The tower was probably used for prayer but the idea of the window was that in the event of being attacked by a Viking, or some other berserker, you and as many other monks that you could muster and perhaps the odd parishioner as well, would take the ladder to the window half way up the tower and then smartly pull the ladder up behind you before they could get near you. There is a very good example of the round tower in St Finian's church in Clonmacnoise and another one, beautifully preserved, in Glendalough, County Wicklow, the Valley of Two Lakes.

The Vikings are often given the credit for destroying and burning most of the towers and the monasteries of Ireland, but some of the fighting Irish tribes of the north and the south did more than their share of burning and pillaging as well. The Vikings knocked

THE ROCK OF CASHEL, CO TIPPERARY

The round tower and ruins of the 13th-century cathedral stand proud on a limestone outcrop.
This is one of Ireland's most historical and therefore most popular sites.

'seven bells' out of Ireland, and indeed, the rest of Europe, for about two hundred years and they founded Ireland's first city, Dublin, on the mouth of the Liffey. The Vikings were defeated by the High King of Ireland, Brian Boru, in the Great Battle of Clontarf on the north side of Dublin Bay in 1014; it is as important a date to the Irish as 1066 is for the English. And so, with the Vikings defeated, Ireland went through another renaissance of art and music and prayer and architecture. In County Tipperary stands the Rock of Cashel from where Brian Boru ruled Munster and subsequently all of Ireland, and where King Cormac built a marvellous chapel on the rock; you can see its remains to this day – the round tower and its high cross, an imposing sight, from its dominating position above the lush pasturelands of Tipperary.

Once in County Tipperary, I drove through on a wet and windy night from Dublin to a little town where I was supposed to pick the Queen of a Harvest Festival or the May Queen – merciful time has erased the memory of exactly what the girl was to be Queen of. It must have been around 9 o'clock when I drove into this windy and rainswept town in Tipperary; not a soul about, the only lights coming from the pubs on the tiny main street. I sat for a moment to collect my thoughts and as I did, a man came out of one of the pubs, and taking his bicycle from the side of the wall, was about to make off into the night, when I said, 'Excuse me, sir, can you tell me where' (whatever the name of the place was) 'is?' He said, 'Ah, I don't know, I'm a stranger here myself.' I wound up the window, and drove on, to find a signpost about a hundred yards further on, which told me that the place I wanted was about three miles away down the road. Where do you think that man had come from, on his bicycle, on that rain-accursed night? Had he cycled from Belfast, just for a drink, to this little Tipperary town? I still think of that and wonder . . . .

I've judged many a beauty contest in my time, when I was a boy broadcaster in Ireland, in various parts of my native land. What used to make it very difficult was that you had to find out very quickly who the local girl was, and if she had any aspirations at all to any passing attractiveness, it was to her that you gave the crown; that is, if you wanted to collect your fee. The Committee would surround you when you arrived, and give you a list of instructions as long as your arm. This Queen of the May, Queen of the Festival, Queen of all that she surveyed, was to be picked not just for her beauty, but for her intelligence, perspicacity, courage, mental agility, loyalty, purity, adharance to the Roman Catholic faith; it didn't make it easy, I can tell you, but as long as you stuck to the one rule of picking the local girl, you were usually all right. I once went to select the Queen of the Limerick Festival, along with the Mayor of Limerick. Once again, it was not a simple matter of picking the best looking girl and saying 'There you are, that'll get you the publicity you want,' no, no, no; we had to grill these girls for hours on end about their ambitions, their lives, their educations, their families. It was extraordinary. I remember asking one contestant for Queen of the Limerick Festival what papers she read. 'I read them all,' she said, 'from cover to cover.' So I said, 'Well, perhaps you'll answer me a simple question, then. What's the capital of France?' She looked at me keenly for a moment and said, 'Um, it's on the tip of my tongue.' The Mayor looked a bit embarrassed. I said, 'It begins with a P.' The contestant's eyes lit up. 'Is it Portugal?' The Mayor looked away. We were in for a long night.

THE RIVER SHANNON FLOWS GRANDLY THROUGH THE CENTRE OF IRELAND ▷

A quiet spot near Meelick in Co Limerick

The Mighty Shannon

Crescent College, Limerick, was where the Jesuits got hold of me when I was nine, which, according to the mythology, was a little late for the moulding. Before that, I had been in the hands of the nuns down by the Shannon, just a little upriver from where the sallies grow. My mother took me there for the first day when I was five and she was somewhat surprised as she was preparing lunch, to hear a knock on the door. It was our hero, thews already more manly than would be seemly in a five year old, fine-featured

*Early evening in Clonderlew
Bay near the mouth of the
river*

*The reedy beds at the edge
of the Shannon*

and fresh-faced, saying 'I'm home.' I had grown tired of school after two hours and decided that enough was enough. I always felt like that about school, but I can only remember kindness, gentleness and the brisk, scrubbed smell of the Salesian Convent, Limerick.

The estuary of the Shannon. Somebody had the bright idea during the last war of using Foynes on the estuary as a landing place for flying boats. I am old enough to remember going down to see these extraordinary monsters on their great floats. Then Shannon Airport grew in international significance, and we had to settle for more mundane planes and runways . . . .

Speaking of Ireland's, indeed, these islands', greatest river, the mighty Shannon is not navigable past Limerick; there are too many rapids and rocks and waterfalls: so you've got to hop over to Killaloe – there you can hire your motor cruiser, or if you like, your row boat, and take off up the lordly Shannon, this great river, the grandest, the longest, the broadest in these islands. The river will take you through marvellous lakes, so big that they have their own storms – it can be as calm as a millpond on the fringes of the lake, and in the middle a minor typhoon can be raging, so, if you're thinking of taking a boat up the Shannon, do so with care, and know your stuff. The River Shannon flows confidently and grandly through the centre of Ireland. More sheer scenery, more

The Meeting of the Waters in the Vale of Avoca, Co Wicklow – made famous by Tom Moore's song of that name.

THANK GOD WE'RE SURROUNDED BY WATER!

There's a marvellous song which I last heard sung by Dominic Behan – sainted brother of the sainted writer – which had a chorus in it, 'Thank God we're surrounded by water!' However, as you can see from these pictures, there is a fair amount of Ireland under water as well.

A bridge over the River Avonbeg in Wicklow

The Torc Waterfall near Killarney in Co Kerry

OVERLEAF *Mannin Bay, Co Galway*

The Ennistymon Cascades in Co Clare

Loch Corrib, Co Galway

lakes, more water than you've ever seen in your life, and more deserted than anybody has the right to expect. It is as if you have a whole inland sea to yourself.

On its banks, and up its streams and tributaries, you'll see and hear the echoes of a not-so-distant past in the great gutted houses of what used to be the Anglo-Irish ascendancy, and in the magnificent ruins of Clonfert and Clonmacnoise, the remnants of Ireland's finest hour. Historically, much more than the artificial partition drawn by Lloyd George between the Province of Ulster and the rest of Ireland, the great river has been Ireland's dividing line. East of it, lie the rich lands and pastures; west of the Shannon, hard ground, rocks, a fruitless land. Across the broad river the hated Cromwell drove the rebellious Irish to 'Hell or Connaught', to privation and, at worst, starvation, while he quelled the rest of the country, and settled its rich lands with his soldiers and those Irish who were prepared to co-operate.

Bars and Bicycles

You may be conscious of the very warp and woof of history on which you sail, as you make your way along the Shannon, but, lest you forget, there'll be plenty of people in the pubs and hostelries, to which your raging thirst will drive you, who will remind you of the river's great and terrible history.

If you are thinking of dropping in for the odd pint (and there's really not much point in going, if you're not . . .) be prepared for the odd sing-song. There are, of course 'singing pubs' all over Ireland, where the general atmosphere resembles nothing so much as

Traditional music in a bar in Howth

THE BLUE LOO BAR IN GLENGARRIF IN CO CORK

When I first saw Mike's wonderful photograph, I couldn't stop laughing. It's really typical.
Mike: 'The strange thing is that I saw exactly the same thing somewhere else, I can't remember where but miles away. Absolutely identical.'
They've probably got a stencil of it. If a thing is worth doing, it's worth doing twice . . . .

Liverpool's 'Kop' at a home game against Everton, but you're likely to hear a song in most pubs along the Shannon, and the more out-of-the-way, the better. I mind well, sitting at a bar somewhere in lovely Leitrim (look, I can't be expected to remember the name of every bar I ever frequented . . .) minding my own business, and thinking of my dinner, when a light tenor voice burst into a come-all-ye, 'They're Cutting the Corn Around Creeslough Today', as tear-jerking an emigrant's lament as you'll ever hear. It took me about five minutes before I could make out who the Count John McCormack impersonator was: a little man, sitting in a dark corner, his cap pulled over his eyes, pint in hand, he sang with his head down without raising his eyes. Self-conscious, embarrassed by attention, wanting no applause – yet he *had* to sing his song . . . . When he'd finished, his drinking companion took him by the hand. The singer never looked up. Nobody applauded. We returned to our drinks, respecting his shyness and his need.

The Shannon will take you up to County Leitrim and back to Killaloe again – but you'll never leave it. Like the country itself, it will call you back . . . .

The Jesuits were dressed in black, as is entirely befitting for the followers of 'the Black Pope', which is what the irreverent always call the head of the Jesuit Order – and they had wings; loose flaps of material that hung from their shoulders. I don't know whether these wings were meant to make them look like black angels, but they certainly had that effect, as they scurried along the corridors from classroom to classroom. Ascetic men, *they* spent a lot of time on bicycles as well; I never saw one of them in a car, and whenever we went to play rugby, our trainer would lead the way, on *his* bicycle.

Most of Ireland was on a bicycle, now that I remember, when I was a kid. Dublin was well known for its bicycles. There were more bicycles in Dublin than you'd find in

THERE ARE BICYCLES EVERYWHERE IN IRELAND

When Mike took these pictures, in Co Kerry, Mr O'Shea couldn't understand what Mike was up to and said, 'I can't see what you're bothering about, there's nothing here but me and my cows.' Mike got talking to him and asked where they were going. 'I'm taking them to market, bloody Common Market.' When Mike started to get some shots closer to, the farmer told him to stop a moment, saying 'Wait, the dog's not laughing.'

Amsterdam. It's all changed now, of course, changed utterly, but a car was quite a rarity. We didn't have a car; we didn't have a *phone* – I could never ring anybody up and ask them what to do when I got lost on the Latin homework, and I often got lost on the Latin homework, let me tell you! I had a very good Latin teacher, well, good for me, because he used to strike terror in my boy's heart. I was so frightened of him that I became extremely good at Latin and have vague recollections of getting something like eighty-nine per cent in my Intermediate Certificate Examinations. Subsequently, when I went to Dublin, I had a very easy-going and kindly Latin Teacher, and I did absolutely nothing. On the other hand, I remember another teacher at Crescent College, merciful time having glossed over his name, who used to *really* frighten the daylights out of me. He had been shell-shocked in the war, I'm not sure *what* war, it could have been the last unpleasantness, but he had this habit of jamming his tongue between his teeth, and rubbing his hands furiously together. This man used to put the heart across me to such an extent that I would get sick every morning before going to school; and maths was not my strongest subject. Understandably, this frightener completely turned me off maths for the rest of my life; and indeed, my children have inherited these genes, without ever seeing the man. So much for nurture against nature.

The Jesuits, for intelligent, highly educated men, seemed to me overly keen on the corporal punishment, and they had a very Jesuitical way of doling it out as well. If you were late for class, or if your homework was incorrect, or if you were misbehaving, the teacher-priest would give you a little docket from his little docket book. It would say, 'T. Wogan, 6 slaps, signed "Father Sadist."' Then at lunchtime, you would queue up behind a lot of other quivering souls, and have the tops of your hands knocked off by a cheery, burly Jesuit who obviously got *his* kicks from offering *your* pain up to God. I would cycle home for lunch (back to the old bicycle again) with my hands throbbing – come back, go to class again and find myself queuing up as I was leaving school – I had permanently swollen hands when I was at Crescent, but then, so did nearly everybody else. I don't think that it in any way marked me – but I've never tried to con my children with that shibboleth: 'schooldays are the happiest days of your life . . . .'

At Crescent College I played rugby from the time I was about ten, and tennis. I didn't play anything like cricket or hockey or any of those Protestant games, and there was no swimming pool, just the rather mouldy old tennis courts and the rugby. 'Garrison' games you see – whereas at the Christian Brothers School on the other side of Limerick, they played the 'Gaelic' Games; but *we*, being good middle-class boys, were being prepared for the Bank and insurance companies and, if we were extremely lucky, the professions.

First Visit to Dublin

I remember one memorable day, when myself, and James and Billy – two bosom buddies – took the train, we must have been all of, ooh, twelve or thirteen and wise in the ways of the world. We took the train from Limerick all the way to Kingsbridge Station, Dublin (it's now called Heuston Station, after Sean Heuston, a local hero who fought and died in the time-honoured way), and went to the Granny's in no. 207 Clonliffe Road, where we had an absolutely slap up feed. Then we got the bus into O'Connell Street, which, unless I am much mistaken, was a first time for old Billy and James; I myself, of course, was steeped in the lore of the metropolis, having gone up there to see my Granny for Christmas and summer holidays since tothood. O'Connell Street had Nelson's Pillar,

KINGSBRIDGE STATION IN DUBLIN

At least, that's what it was called then; it's now Heuston Station

The house in Clonliffe Road, Dublin

which was still standing then. The IRA blew it up subsequently. I was in hospital at the time, having caught appendicitis, which the doctors seemed unable to diagnose. The appendix, tired of being ignored, burst, and turned smartly into peritonitis, causing severe fright, and not a little pain. Peritonitis is no fun, and let nobody tell you otherwise. I was lying in my bed of pain, in the Mater Hospital, Dublin, at about 11 o'clock that memorable night in '66, when there was this enormous explosion, and that was it, the end of the old 'one-eyed adulterer' – which is what the Irish have always called Nelson with a great deal of affection; at least I *think* it's affection . . . . Some idiot thought he would strike a blow for Irish independence, nationalism, pride and general anarchy, and blow down the poor innocent statue, which, incidentally, you could climb up the middle of – I climbed up, thank goodness, before your man took it down the hard way, and got up to the top. It was the highest I had ever been in my life, at the time, and you could see all over Dublin. I have since, in my world-weary way, been up the Eiffel Tower, but it has not made me blasé about Nelson's Pillar, particularly as the Eiffel Tower is still standing and, as I have already told you, Nelson's Pillar has gone to dust; there is nothing there now . . . .

Outside Nelson's Pillar, me and Billy and James got a tram – there were trams then, must have been the 50s. Wonderful trams, running on rails, and overhead cables, and we took the tram out to Ballsbridge, and joined the jostling millions, well it seemed like millions, to go and see Ireland play England at the rugby, at Lansdowne Road. I don't know *when* it was in the 50s and I'm not going to look it up; it's not written down anywhere anyway. It rained, I remember that, but we had a wonderful day, although I

O'CONNELL STREET IN DUBLIN

Nelson's Pillar stood in O'Connell Street until the IRA blew it up; this is the statue to Charles Stewart Parnell

don't even remember whether Ireland beat England. We took the train back from Kingsbridge, having had high tea at the Granny's, and I'm sure we were back in Limerick about 9 o'clock – but that day has always seemed to me endless and joyous, one of the great days of my life.

CURIOUS NAMES

Wogans Ideal Home Centre in Dunleer near Drogheda: Wogan is, as everyone knows, a rare and beautiful name and can only be found in the most select localities – mostly in Wales where the family originally came from but there are a fair few Wogans to be found in Co Louth especially in the town of Dunleer where the family appears to have taken over.

Mr W. O'Looney's bar in Kilrush, Co Clare

The Mick Finn bar in Clonakilty, Co Cork. I don't know whether this is the place where the original Mickey Finn was supplied, but it wouldn't surprise me.

Painted Walls

Wall painting is a new thing. I remember very little being done, not even graffiti, in my youth, but it has obviously become a major art form in the last few years.

Tralee, Co Kerry

Ballydehob in Co Cork

Carlingford, Co Louth

Fishing Days

Limerick sits astride the broad grey Shannon, with King John and his castle on one side and J. Arthur Rank and his slightly less historic mills on the other. In those far-off days, Limerick wasn't big on mills, factories or any kind of industry. I can only remember a toffee factory (I blame my sweet tooth on an early smell of the place while being walked by in my pram), cigarette factory (Craven 'A', with the red box and a black cat's face on the front. Gone, gone and never called me mother . . .) and a cement factory. I remember the cement factory very well, because I used to pass it every Sunday, on the crossbar of my father's bicycle, as he took me fishing on the Maigue, a tributary of the Shannon.

FISHING WEEKENDS

I used to go fishing with my father almost every weekend during my formative years.

RIGHT *Ferry Bridge on the River Maigue: the very place where we fished and caught all those eels. I would have crossed that bridge hundreds of times. It reminds me of the call of the corncrake: 'Ate bacon! Ate bacon!'*

The Maigue is a tributary of the Shannon, and I graduated to fishing on the Shannon when I got bigger.

The waterwheel at Croom, also on the River Maigue

Most of the weekends of my formative years seem now to have been spent on the banks of the muddy Maigue. I don't remember any great creels of fish being landed; perhaps the very occasional trout and the odd flounder; lots of eels, but they had to go back, as my mother wouldn't touch them with a barge-pole. Later on, as my father marched up the grocer's and victualler's ladder, we acquired a car, and our fishing expeditions took on a less riparian flavour, as he cast his hook into the Atlantic breakers at Quilty, on the Clare coast. That was much better for a growing lad, with the dunes and the beach, and the sandwiches of corned beef and Limerick ham. The old man didn't catch much by the sea-shore either, apart from a suicidal mackerel or a careless bass. It was the getting-ready that counted with my father, not the fishing itself. I would spend countless hours digging up rag-worms (between the worm-cast and the hole, that's where they were. Dig down, and you'd find yourself with something that looked more like a grass snake than a worm. That never worried me, though. Hadn't St Patrick got rid of snakes?) My father, meanwhile, would prepare endlessly; and as the sun was going down behind the dunes, he would finally be ready to do battle with the breakers. A couple of casts, then it was time to pack up and go home . . . .

Quilty, like most places in Clare, was the next best thing to New York, well the next parish anyway – a step across the broad Atlantic and there you were, Manhattan. Quilty was deserted then, with just a few fishermen. It's still deserted now, with the same fishermen . . . .

QUILTY, CO CLARE

The seaweed which gathers on the shore at Quilty is dried for kelp-making.

Seafield Harbour looking towards the Quilty sand dunes, where the Wogan family shared many a fly-infested picnic . . . .

Cottages

There is a romantic idea, that probably grew to its full flowering with The Quiet Man *and Maureen O'Hara in her red petticoats, that the average Irishman lived in a pretty, sparkling white thatched cottage. However, the majority of Irish peasants lived in not much more than a mud hut rather than a stone cottage.*

GOOD, GOOD, GOING, GONE . . . .

A thatched cottage with a pretty garden in Adare, Co Limerick

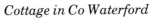
Cottage in Co Waterford

A ruined roadside house in Co Cork which is
now used as a hay store

A ruined cottage under Twelve Bens in
Connemara

Summers at Lahinch and Kilkee

I have a very soft spot for Clare, for very many reasons. A great friend of mine, Michael Clancy, had a house in Lahinch, between the two golf courses. Many's the time I went down there, and joined him and his wife and family and his friends; and we would play the course. Or rather *he* would play, and I would attempt to battle my way through the wind and the rain and the hard pounding of an Atlantic-lashed Irish summer. It's hard to know the best time of year to visit Lahinch – some say Christmas, because it's not quite as cold there as anywhere else in Europe, but summer is certainly not the time, because there is a fair amount of wind and rain lashing in, between the occasional burst of sunshine. There's a wide and curving beach at Lahinch, one of the great beaches of Europe, and after being pounded to a pulp by the Atlantic surf, you can further exhaust yourself by playing golf on one of the great courses of the world.

The goats are one of the main features of the course – you have got to keep a shrewd weather-eye on the goats. When they are sheltering beneath the eaves of the Club House, it is a very foolish man who takes his clubs and launches himself into the Force 9 gale up the First. The goats know better. But when the creatures are out in the country – feel free, pick up your cleek, your mashie and your rib-faced niblick and off you go. Mind you, you have to be a fair golfer because Lahinch doesn't take any prisoners. I remember playing golf with Michael, one memorable morning, when we had partaken, as was his custom, of rashers and eggs and black pudding, and some white pudding and mushrooms, and perhaps a taste or two of smoked salmon to start, and that was only breakfast. There had been some fried bread, and brown bread, and soda bread, and coffee, and tea, and porridge, to give some ballast. As we were marching into the wind I said to Michael, 'My goodness, an extraordinary thing, old comrade, but I feel like a stuck pig.' 'Listen,' he said, 'Lahinch is no place to be playing hungry golf.' You could not but agree with him.

There are some holes in Lahinch, indeed *most* holes, as I recollect, where even as you stand on the tee, you can see nothing, zippo. It's not just the rain blinding you, there isn't a green in sight. You *can* see little white markers stuck up on four mile high sand dunes and hills; you are supposed to hit over these markers, and go on in that general direction until the green and the pin expose themselves to you. A couple of years ago an American visitor, hitting for a short hole, with an invisible green, and an invisible flag sited in an invisible hole, struck the ball fairly well, and landed up on the green to find, to his delight, that the ball was nestling in the hole! He reached into his back pocket and crowned his caddy with a $50 note. It *rained* money on the caddy. It is said that after that, visiting Americans had holes in one on this particular green with astounding frequency, until the Greens Committee cottoned on to what was going on. Frankly, as a pretty duff golfer, I feel that this sort of creative caddying should not be discouraged.

The Harbour at Liscannor, Co Clare

The currachs, which are made from tarred canvas stretched over a wooden frame, are still used along the west coast of Ireland, and in the Aran Islands.

OVERLEAF *Lahinch has one of the great beaches of Europe and one of the great golf courses of the world, side by side. Look at the cloud formations in these two photographs. You never get tired of Irish weather. It doesn't give you a chance. It can change while you're looking around you . . . .*

Up a bit, and round the bay from Lahinch, past Liscannor Bay, are the Cliffs of Moher, where the land simply gives up, decides it's had enough, and drops everything into the Atlantic – a spectacular place. If you continue along far enough, you will come to Galway Bay which is the place to be, in the words of the song, 'if you ever go across to Ireland, and it may be at the closing of your day'. A lot of Irish songs deal freely in matters of scenery and the class of things which they properly feel ought to be praised to the skies, though why you have to wait until your day closes, has never been clear to me . . . .

But before I leave Clare . . . when I was a lad, with my friend Billy, we used to go to Kilkee, a popular holiday resort for the Irish, with a little crescent beach, absolutely ideal for swimming, except, as I recall, nobody used to swim off it, because there were so many other places to swim, and it was too *easy* to swim off the beach; it wasn't done, anyway, in those puritanical days of the 50s, to undress there, in full view of the passing parade. If you hadn't a house overlooking the beach in which you could undress, then I'm afraid your chances of having a dip were very sparse indeed, if you cared at all for the opinions of your fellow holiday-makers. For Kilkee was Limerick-by-the-Sea, and carried with it the same conservative traditions of that very religious city.

There was a routine about going there on holiday. Of a morning, Billy and I would spring lightly from our beds (this *was* a long time ago), look out at the driving rain, reach for our bathing togs, and then march purposefully around the headland to Burns' Cove. A tiny little harbour with two little quays, through which, if the tide was right, and the wind in the right direction, you might squeeze a currach. We would fling ourselves off one quay, and swim smartly across to the steps of the other. My one clear recollection is the cold, the biting cold of it. It seemed to me that the warming waters of the Gulf Stream, of which we used to hear about so much in our Irish Geography classes, bringing as it did, mild calm and soft weather to Ireland, missed Burns' Cove completely. The water was enough to freeze the gonads but, you *had* to have a swim – you'd walked around the bay for about a mile and a half and when you got there, there was nothing else to do *except* swim. The cove was a semi-nude bathing place, women were *not* encouraged, because the occasional man would divest himself and spring into the non-Gulf Stream waters like a good'un, naked as a Jay bird, and come out, of course, with everything blue, and teeth chattering. Occasionally, there would be bursts of girlish laughter from the cliff tops where the more spritely of the holidaying Limerick ladies had come round to the cove, to have a good laugh at the shrivelled nudity of their fellow-townsmen. We didn't care, Burns' Cove was ours, cold, jellyfish and all. Then we'd walk back, the blood slowly returning to our frozen veins, just in time for lunch. After lunch, we *had* to go to the Pollock Holes. The Pollock Holes were three in number. The first was where *women* were allowed to swim, and small children – it was extremely shallow and safe, and providing you didn't get the odd stinging anemone shoving its

THE CLIFFS OF MOHER

PREVIOUS PAGE *This is one of the best stretches of cliffs in the whole of the British Isles. Made of dark sandstone, they drop sheer into the Atlantic.*

THE SHORE OF GALWAY BAY

KILKEE IN CO CLARE

Kilkee stands on the crescent-shaped Moore Bay.

little shafts up your toes, you were perfectly all right. Then if you walked another fifty yards you came to the Second Pollock Hole – nothing very exciting there and, once again, liberal thinkers turned a tolerant eye to young women swimming *there*. Fair enough. A little further on, there was a line drawn on the rock, which clearly stated: 'No women beyond this point'. The Third Pollock Hole was the last bastion of male supremacy, and nudity. You were bloody nothing if you didn't take your togs off at the Third Pollock Hole. I don't remember a great deal of resentment amongst the women, although I would be very surprised if that line still exists. There's a different class of woman abroad these days, and Ireland is no exception.

Kilkee was where I learned to dance. I suppose one of the reasons I was fit to compère 'Come Dancing' was my aptitude for the foxtrot, the quickstep and slow waltz, learned assiduously in the ballroom of the Hydro Hotel, Kilkee. It wasn't like today you see, when you can get out there and shake a tail feather with the best of them, according to your manly, or indeed, womanly instincts. From watching Kev and Trace on 'Top of the Pops' you can get a good idea of how to Shake That Thing. It wasn't the same in our day, you had to be able to do the old one two and one two, or one two three, one two three. One of my aunts gave me a book of Victor Sylvester's, with little footprints, with arrows, and dotted lines between them. I could make neither head nor tail of it. However, Billy's sister taught me how to dance, and providing I could keep the old count going I didn't acquit myself at all badly at the occasional *thé dansant* that used to go on at the Hydro.

A short cut across Kilkee's lovely beach

Collin's Medical Hall – or what most people call a chemist's and what my Great-Aunt Mag used to call an 'apothecary'.

Talking of dancing, at the Crescent College, they used to have 'school dances'. This was an enormous breakthrough, in the 50s in Ireland. We were allowed to tread a measure with the girls from Laurel Hill Convent, no others; we were the two middle-class schools, so we were allowed to dance with one another – girls on one side of the hall, boys on the other. These dances were scarcely evenings of unalloyed pleasure, because the place was infested with priests and nuns. You couldn't get within an ass's roar of your partner. It was rather like modern dancing, so perhaps nothing's changed a great deal, and I didn't miss as much as I thought at the time.

I remember my most embarrassing moment was going into the newsagent's in Kilkee and standing quite near a girl to whom I had taken an enormous fancy. As I bent down surreptitiously to look at the *Beano*, all the accumulations of water that had been stored in my sinuses, from diving into Burns' Cove and the Third Pollock Hole came rushing out, splattering all over the linoleum floor. That girl never looked at me in quite the same way again.

Dublin I

The sainted woman who calls me 'son', and who is known to the rest of the family as 'rough-house Rosie', was born in Belfast, one of two daughters of 'Muds', and Frank Byrne, a sergeant-major in the British Army, who had fought in the Boer War. I only remember him as a waxed moustache, for he died when I was very young. 'Muds' was a frail, gentle and very deaf old lady, the whistle from whose hearing-aid frightened many a passing horse and cart. 'Muds', or if you like, the Granny, came from a generation and a time not that far gone, when Dublin was more of a village than a city. She epitomised a song you may hear in many a Liffey-side pub, 'I Remember Dear Old Dublin in the Rare Old Times', in which the singer bemoans the events that have made 'A City of my Town'. The place was even smaller when my Granny was a girl, long before Joyce sent Bloom across the city in search of his breakfast. Mention a name to the old lady, and she could trace the family tree for you, as could her elder sister, my great-aunt Mag, who lived with her. Mag was a formidable maiden lady, a former trade union organiser, and a 'french-polisher' of high renown. She could remember the whistle of the bullets as she passed the G.P.O. during the Easter Rising of 1916. Muds and Mag would sing funny little bits of old Dublin street-songs and cries, as they dandled me on their knees, or in later years, lightly cuffed me behind the ears: 'St James' Street May Trip You – and Not Forgettin' the Fountain!' was one of their favourites for which I'm sure only the great Eamonn MacThomais would have an explanation. 'There's Goin' up Cork Hill!' was another, and my own favourite, 'Billy in the Bowl, and that's it all!' I happened to come across an explanation of this latter chant a few years ago. 'Billy in the Bowl!' was a famous Dublin crippled beggar of the last century. He propelled himself about the town in a little bowl with wheels, begging for food or money. A popular figure, until it was discovered that the bold Billy wasn't just begging for money. In dark alleyways, with his powerful arms, he was strangling people for it, as well . . . . The Irish cherish their 'characters', luckily few of them are as murderous as 'Billy in the Bowl'. Although the one I remember clearly from my youth was firmly convinced that he was wiping out a fair cross-section of the population as well. He was known to all and sundry as 'Bang-Bang'. A wild, dishevelled figure in a raincoat, he took free trips all over Dublin on the platforms of buses, leaning out with a comb or a piece of stick in his hand, 'shooting' everything that moved, while shouting, 'Bang! Bang!' at the top of his voice. A pretty nasty turn he could give you, if you didn't hear him coming . . . . He did it for years, under the kindly patronage of Dublin's bus conductors. Nobody ever stopped him, chastised him, or as far as I know, attempted to put him away. When he died the city mourned . . . .

Moore Street, the open market just a short step from O'Connell Street, was full of 'characters', and people would go down there just to hear the banter and badinage of

Two Contrasting Markets

ABOVE *The open market in Moore Street in Dublin, and* BELOW *the rather less official one in Kilrush, a market town in Co Clare. In little Irish country towns like Kilrush, the markets just seem to appear.*

traders, as they do in London's Petticoat Lane. A much-loved figure was 'Rosie', a rotund, jolly woman with a tongue like an adder. My mother recounts Rosie's retort to a woman who complained about the price of the fresh mackerel: 'Whaddya want for sixpence – Moby Dick?'!

Another famous Dubliner was a certain Deputy Lord Mayor, about whom the stories are legion: on one occasion, in the absence of the incumbent, our friend was deputised to greet the great Halle Orchestra with their conductor, Sir John Barbirolli, on the steps of Dublin's Mansion House, which stands resplendent on Dawson Street, near St Stephen's Green, the best place in Dublin for ducks and watching the world go by.

'I know you will join me,' intoned the Deputy Lord Mayor, in his flat Dublin tones, exacerbated by a marked lisp, 'in extending a hearty *Céad Míle Fáilte,* a hundred thousand Irish welcomes, to our visitors: Sir John Barolli and his Band . . .'!

Another tale of this great man tells of an impassioned plea made on behalf of blind children. 'I know,' he cried emotionally to a packed audience, 'all too well the problems of the blind! Haven't I got three blind children at home?!' After the speech, which was no less emotionally received by the crowd, a relative rushed to his side. 'Lorcan!' said the relative, 'what are you talking about? You haven't got any blind children!' 'I know, I know,' answered our Lord. 'I got carried away . . . .'

Although my mother was born in Belfast, regretfully my knowledge of that great Victorian city is sketchy. I only ever travelled there on a couple of occasions to play rugby, and similarly, ashamed as I am to admit it, I know nothing of the beauties of Northern Ireland or Ulster, because I have never been there. Mind you, as you will readily gather from this book, there are many places in Ireland I have never visited. But then, small and all as it looks on the map, Ireland's a big place if you've only got a bicycle . . . . So my apologies here and now to the counties and places of which my knowledge is sketchy, not to say non-existent.

POWERSCOURT CENTRE,
OFF GRAFTON STREET

I know from what Mike has told me that the Powerscourt Centre is a modern but gracious and very colourful shopping precinct. I think this is a splendid example of how these things can be done. It is a place full of light, movement and live music.

DUBLIN

The Irish call it 'Dublinn' – the Dark Pool, from the dark, peat-coloured waters of the Liffey. The Norse called it Dyfflin, and the Anglo-Normans Dublinne. To the Granny though, it was just 'Dear Old Dirty Dublin' . . . .

Donagh MacDonagh, a judge, poet and playwright, in a poem called 'Dublin Made Me', sums up the true 'Dub's' attitude to the rest of the country:

> *I disclaim all fertile meadows, all tilled land*
> *The evil that grows from it and the good,*
> *But the Dublin of old Statutes, this arrogant city,*
> *Stirs proudly and secretly in my blood.*

THE ILAC CENTRE

Here mothers can leave their children when they want to go off shopping; someone dressed, say, like Snow White will read the children stories and keep them amused and happy.

RIGHT *A lamp on a bridge over the Liffey and* BELOW *a pair of perfect Georgian doorways*

PHOENIX PARK

The Irish claim that Phoenix Park is the largest walled park in Europe.

SUNRISE AND EARLY MORNING

*Dublin Docks near the Custom House and the docks on the Grand Canal near the mouth of the
River Liffey*

Irish Sport

RACING

Father, as I've already told you, was a 'Garden of Ireland', a Wicklow man. He learned to fly-fish for trout in the streams and mountain lakes of his beautiful native county, but all too soon was packed off to the grocer's curateship in Bray, and thence to Dublin, from where he was promoted to the awesome heights of managing a small grocer's shop in O'Connell Street, Limerick, for the long-since departed high-class victualling firm of Leverette and Frye. There was plenty of high-class victualling required too, surprisingly enough, in that small Irish city (the third biggest in Ireland, if you didn't count Belfast, and don't you forget it . . .). The somewhat faded remnants of Anglo-Irish gentry were still about. 'The Relics of ould decenty' and the 'remittance' men, the usually disgraced sons of English nobility who had been despatched by enraged parents from their native shires to a couple of thousand acres of prime Irish farmland, and a regular 'remittance' from Blighty, just so long as they stayed away. These people had a long-developed taste for fine wines, viands and comestibles, and my father kept them liberally supplied. As he did the 'horsey' set. In a land where only God takes precedence over the horse, Limerick and Tipperary (oh all right, Kildare as well), are acknowledged as the premier counties for the breeding and rearing of the finest horse-flesh in the world. Rarely did my father come home without some kind of a tip for the races at Limerick Junction, the Curragh or Leopardstown. Luckily enough, equally rarely did he bother to back anything. He knew his stuff, though. In his declining years, he came with me to a friend's box at Ascot, and went through the card . . . .

A keen punter, the old man, but through a maze of each way doubles and trebles he never seemed to expend more than 2s 6d. In the great tradition of all British and Irish offshore punters, he didn't actually attend race meetings, and it was really one of the joys of my life that I was able to bring him, in his declining years, to places like Ascot and Newbury and Windsor. But, of course, he was completely lost; he'd never gone to race meetings in Ireland, he'd gone into the bookies.

Bookies, he understood, but the race course itself, the tic-tac men, the hustle and the bustle, the heckling and the betting on numbers, instead of the names, on the Tote, totally confused him. He enjoyed the people, I think, more than the horses, much as I do myself; with a couple of glasses of Right Stuff inside him, my father at a race meeting became known as 'the Kissing Bandit'. He wasn't much of a one for a torrid embrace in his sober moments, but the Old Man was a terror with the champagne lapping up against his back teeth; he kissed everyone – those who were lucky enough to escape on the basis of gender or foreign aspect were engaged in fine-sounding talk.

I mind well the occasion at Windsor, when the old boy trapped an unwary Chinese gentleman and questioned him closely on the Communist government and, specifically, Mao. Since the gentleman was a member of the Hong Kong Jockey Club, and probably had never been to the Chinese mainland in his life, and my father insisted on pronouncing Mao, M–A–Y–O, you hardly need me to describe how confusing the conversation became. I didn't intervene, for fear that the old Kissing Bandit would turn his attention on some poor unsuspecting Dowager.

My father saw no need to induce me or introduce me in my formative years to the pleasures of the Irish racetrack. I do have, though, a vague recollection of being taken by bus to the Irish Grand National at Fairyhouse when I was scarcely out of my knee breeches. I was taken by my kindly Uncle Eddie – how in Heaven's name he saw fit to lumber himself with a muling and indeed puking infant, I will never understand. We left by bus, and bus journeys always upset my stomach. So did car journeys, incidentally, but we didn't have a car; I could sit on a bicycle forever without getting sick. This good man took me to the Irish Grand National for reasons that must remain a mystery. He was rewarded, however, for his kindness and, indeed, his endurance because we backed the winner. I can remember the winner's name to this day: Alberoni. I can remember being sick on the bus, of course, there and back, but nothing else. . . .

It was a considerable number of years before I chanced my stomach at another race meeting, and indeed I had a car by then. That was in Dublin, and there still weren't that many cars in Dublin when I was a lad, or when I was a boy in the bank, me and my Morris Minor with the broken passenger seat. I must have been all of about twenty, when, pursuant to my policy of becoming the Burlington Bertie of Grafton Street, and Lothario-in-chief of the Dublin coffee bar set, I took a couple of girls, well bred, mind you, along in my Morris Minor – one of them had to sit in the back, well actually both sat in the back, because the broken passenger seat was really no place to be sitting if you valued your life – to the Mecca of Dublin's racing society, the Phoenix Park. I must be getting older than even you think, because I can recall little about that meeting either; the girls' faces aren't even a hazy memory – it could have been the drink, of course. People were dressed in their best, the men dressing for the benefit and of approval of the women and the women dressing for the benefit and approval of the women. The other thing that sticks in my memory about Phoenix Park, was that you never knew who won any of the races until it was announced over the public address system – the finishing post was out of sight of the enclosure and most of the stands. The horses would belt hell for leather past the corner of the main stand, and were seen no more. A great cheer would greet the unseen winner and everybody held on to their tickets until the announcement was made. Some may think it is peculiarly Irish to have a winning post that none of the paying customers could see, but it certainly added a frisson to the day. Nobody cared anyway; you don't go to watch the races to win money in Ireland, you go for the crack.

SOCCER

My father went to the dogs twice a week, in the evenings to the Markets Field, Limerick. Small bets; he never risked the family jewels, even if we'd had any, apart from my mother's engagement ring. The Markets Field was also where Limerick soccer team played. Many an epic League of Ireland struggle did I watch there against Shamrock Rovers, or Bohemians, or Cork Athletic. There's no Cork Athletic anymore, it's called Cork something else. Bohemians and Shamrock Rovers are still there; Limerick F.C. has been called several things since I've been gone. Ah, my heroes, my O'Grady's, my Collopys of long ago. There was a fellow who used to play on the wing for Limerick, a speedy little chap who used to wear shorts rather like Stanley Matthews' – baggy and knee length – that was what endeared him to me and the Limerick crowd. They called him 'Mugua, after the Last of the Mohicans. Maybe he was . . . .

My real footballing heroes, though, in common with most Irish youngsters then and now, were far across the Irish Sea, and playing for teams like Manchester United, Everton and Blackpool. Heroes with names such as Carey and Farr, Matthews and Mortensen. Because I went to the Jesuit, rather than the Christian Brothers College in Limerick, my interests as a player and spectator were what the more 'nationally' minded referred to as 'garrison' games, games introduced to previously unsullied Holy Catholic and Gaelic Ireland by the rough British soldiery. Football, rugby and hockey were garrison games. There must have been a question mark over tennis and netball as well. And don't talk to me about cricket. . . . Me and the boys had another, even more intense interest, table football – Subbuteo. We all had our little table football teams. I was the first with one; I used to play table football with myself on the carpet, in the Good Room. You see I was an only child for six years, that makes you lean on yourself quite a lot. I've always enjoyed my own company best – I suspect that's why I enjoy radio, which is really only talking to yourself. Table football was the game, we even had a league, me and Jim and Bill (well, Billy, but he changed it to Bill when he was a bit older) and John and Jim's brother and we all had our teams. We had several teams each, all English: Hull City, Wigan, Corinthian Casuals, Sheffield Wednesday, Wolves, Tottenham Hotspur, Manchester United. We'd go round with our little plastic teams in a cardboard box and play each other at table football. For a year, or so, it took up all our time. I never knew how I got my homework done; well I didn't really, but you had to get your priorities right, table football was the thing.

THE GAMES OF THE GAEL

On the other side of Limerick, over the Sarsfield Bridge and out on the Ennis Road, was the Gaelic Athletic Ground. Here the noble and truly 'Irish' games of hurling and Gaelic football were played, local and inter-county level. There's nothing historic nor natively 'Gaelic' about the football – the game was invented about a hundred years ago to take the minds of honest Irish youths off the contaminated garrison games of soccer and rugby, but its inspiration comes mainly from those two hated English games. Gaelic football is played with a soccer ball and rugby goalposts, but you can't run more than a few steps with the ball in your hands and there's no tackling. I'm sure it was the inspiration for Australian Rules football which it closely resembles, except, of course, *that's* played with a rugby ball, two sets of goal posts and on an oval pitch. . . .

Hurling's the true game of the Gael. There's nothing quite like it, unless you count hockey – and you'd better not, at least in the environs of a hurling fan. It's played with hurling sticks, or in Gaelic 'camans', and a hard, pigskin ball called the 'sliothar'. It's reputed to be the fastest field game in the west and it's also extremely skilful and dangerous. Nowadays, most of the participants wear hard hats like cyclists, or cricketers, to prevent contusions to the cranium caused by flying camans, but in the days of my youth, I saw many a gladiator led from the field with his head opened. However, a few words from his local parish priest, a lick of the magic sponge and our hero would bound back on again, swathed in bandages and looking pale but determined . . . .

When I was in my formative years, the great heroes of the Limerick team came from a place called Ahane. The Mackeys they were called, there was Mick and there was John, and Mick was a legendary hurler, a marvellously skilful, somewhat overweight gentleman, I remember, but maybe I was seeing him in his declining years. There was always a tremendous argument between Limerick and Cork people about who was the better; Mick Mackey, the legendary Limerick man, or Christy Ring, the legendary Cork man. Even though I'm a Limerick man, I'd say Christy Ring had the edge: his career lasted longer. He was a remarkable hurler, a balding gnome of a man. He used to drive a lorry for some petrol company and when he felt the urge he would stop his lorry and get out and puck a few balls up and down a field; that was all the training he ever did, but he had inordinate skills.

Up until quite recently, the Gaelic Athletic Association expressly forbade all those who played its great Irish games from playing the hated English ones. You could be summarily expelled, never to lift your caman in the company of a decent Irishman again, if you so much as attended a rugby match. Gaelic footballers and hurlers played soccer under assumed names, lest they brought disgrace on themselves and their families. As my sainted Granny used to say, 'Where else would you get it, but in Ireland . . . ?'

Notwithstanding the memory of such jingoistic lunacy, the traveller who would seek to imbibe deeply at the Irish spring, need look no further than an inter-county Gaelic football or hurling match at any of the big provincial grounds; or, if you can beg, borrow or steal a ticket, an All Ireland semi-final or final, at the holy of holies of Gaelic athleticdom, Croke Park, Dublin. There you will see Ireland assembled: prelate, priest, doctor, docker, bank clerk and farmer, pipe bands, marching bands and the ball thrown in to start the game by the President of Ireland, no less. Incidentally, with a fine disregard for the sharper end of prejudice, the President and Prime Minister also traditionally attend Irish Rugby Internationals at Lansdowne Road, Dublin on the south side of the Liffey. While bowing to nobody in their regard for the President, Republicanism runs strongly through most Irishmen's veins, and there is in all of us, a marked reluctance to bend the knee. The Irish like to bring everybody down to their own size, and, in the case of one particular President, Sean T. O'Ceallaigh, it wasn't difficult. For the man was little over five feet tall. I will not easily forget standing on the terraces at Lansdowne Road, when the bold Sean T. walked on to the field to inspect the players. Resplendent in Homburg hat and Crombie coat, the tiny figure marched on, as the crowd chanted cheerily: 'Cut the Grass! Cut the Grass!'

But to return to the Mecca of Gaelic sport, Croke Park. The Irish are often portrayed as a warlike people, always ready and willing for a fight. Partial, I may be, with even a hint of bias, but I have been here and there a bit, and I find the Irish the least aggressive of races. Amongst the hundred thousand highly excited and partisan supporters at Croke Park, you find nothing but smiles and songs and laughter. No vile chants, no violence, no crowd scenes. The mayhem on the pitch finds no reflection in the sweetness and light of the crowd. Hymns are sung, anthems are proudly intoned, bands are cheered, and even the opposition gets applauded if it has played fairly and well. The Irish, en masse, are a credit to themselves . . . .

Phoenix Park

On any Sunday in Phoenix Park, you will find strollers, footballers, hurlers, deer, lovers, drinkers, picnickers. The great meeting point is the Wellington Memorial. (Why they blew up Nelson's Pillar and not Wellington's Monument remains a mystery! Maybe because Wellington was a Dublin man himself . . . .) I used to meet my friends here on a Sunday and we'd pick two teams for football and play on the broad expanses of parkland. °

Ancient Ireland

The 'Gaels' were the Celtic tribe that settled and conquered not only Ireland, but Scotland and northern France, bringing with them iron swords and iron ploughshares, six centuries or so before Christ. It was they that called the country 'Erin' and they dominated it for over thirteen hundred years, until the Vikings challenged their supremacy. But the remarkable thing is that Celtic/Gaelic culture remained the dominant influence in Ireland well into the eighteenth century, and relics and fortresses can still be seen wherever you go, in Erin. At Tara in County Meath, for instance, the seat of the High King of Ireland, where in the third century AD, the then High King ('Ard-Ri' in Gaelic), Cormac MacAirt, built schools for the study of literature, the law, and war. And an enormous palace, with a banqueting hall seven hundred feet long. Throughout the centuries, Tara was a rallying point for the Gael, and even in 1843, a million people gathered there, to hear the Liberator, Daniel O'Connell, speak . . . .

The pride of Tara is long gone now, as the nineteenth-century Irish poet, Thomas Moore so poignantly puts it:

> The harp that once through Tara's hall
> The soul of music shed
> Now hangs as mute on Tara's walls
> As if that soul were fled . . . .

Before the Gaels were the Neolithic Irishmen, whose passage graves, burial chambers and dolmens still dot the country. The dolmen of Browne's Hill in County Carlow has a capstone of over a hundred tons; even today, McAlpine's Fusiliers would have a tough job lifting *that* into place. A passage grave at Newgrange in County Meath, dating from about 2500 BC is still in a remarkable state of preservation, and can be seen to have been designed by its builders so that the sun could penetrate into the burial chamber itself only once a year, on Midwinter's Day. I've called into that burial chamber myself; not a trip for the over-large nor the claustrophobic. I must have been a good deal younger when I did it.

Who these people were who could build such tombs and display such knowledge of astronomy, or indeed, where they came from, remains largely a mystery to the historian, but not to the ancient storytellers of Ireland's myths or sagas. According to them, the first people to set foot in the place were the Formorians, an extremely nasty crowd led by Balor of the Evil Eye, who could shrivel an Irish elk at a glance. The Giant's Causeway in Country Antrim was their stairway (a later saga says Finn McCool threw it there in a fit of pique, but let me not confuse you . . .) and the dark, threatening Tory Island, off the coast of Donegal, was their home. Then there were the Partholonians, the

Fortresses and Castles

Castles were part and parcel of growing up in Ireland; they were everywhere and just got taken for granted. Living as I did in Limerick, which was a Norman stronghold, ruined castles were part of my youth. Bunratty Castle and King John's Castle were two that I remember visiting.

Carrigogunnell Castle

This is close to the estuary of the Shannon, just outside Limerick.

Castle Trim

ABOVE *Castle Trim in Co Meath is a vast 16-sided fort, and was once Ireland's strongest Norman fortress.*

Kildaunet Castle

This stands on Achill Island in Co Mayo and was a vital fortress in its heyday.

KING JOHN'S CASTLE

This castle stands on the banks of the mighty Shannon at Limerick.

CASTLE ADARE

The magnificent ruins of the friary and Adare castle on the banks of the River Maigue in Co Limerick.

TIMOLEAGUE CASTLE

OVERLEAF *Set between Kinsale and Clonakilty in Co Cork, this castle looks south across the sea.*

Ireland's Prehistory

A

B

C

ABOVE *The Proleek Dolmen stands on the Cooley Peninsula in Co Louth.*

A *Creevykeel in Co Sligo is one of Ireland's best examples of a chambered tomb.*

B *This dolmen at Browne's Hill, just outside Carlow, has a capstone weighing around 100 tons.*

C *The Burren in Co Clare has a wealth of prehistoric monuments, specifically the Poulnabrone portal dolmen and the Poulaphuca wedge tomb. The dolmen shown in this photographs is about 2½ feet high and a number of them can be found around the Poulnabrone dolmen – but they aren't prehistoric: they have been made recently by young aspiring architects.*

<u>The Dromberg Stone Circle</u>

PREVIOUS PAGE AND ABOVE *This lies between Clonakilty and Skibbereen in Co Cork and is one of Ireland's answers to Stonehenge.*

Nemedians, and my favourites, the Fir Bolgs. The Fir Bolgs ('Bag Men' in English) were reputedly so called because they were descended from the poor unfortunates who carried up the bagfuls of bricks that made the pyramids! It gives an added piquancy to a song of the early 50s of Ray Ellington's that went:

> It must have been the Irish
> That built the Pyramids
> 'Cos no one else
> Could carry up the bricks . . . .

The Fir Bolgs got the works in their turn from the Tuatha de Danaan, who had magic on their side, and an unbeaten battler called Lugh of The Long Arm.

Traditionally, the Fir Bolgs' last stand was at Dun Aengus, the fortress which can still be seen on Inishmore, the biggest of the Aran Islands. The Tuatha de Danaan got it in the neck from the last settlers of the saga, the Milesians (not to be confused with the Salesians, that grand crowd of nuns who tried to beat some sense into me when I was but a tot – without much success, as history records . . .). These Milesians had a poet, who went north, and a harpist, who went south. To this day, Ireland's poets come from the North, its singers and songs from the South . . . more or less . . . !

The Aran Islands, off the coast of Galway, have long been seen as the last bastion of truly Gaelic culture, with their Irish-speaking inhabitants, and a way of life that has scarcely changed for hundreds of years. The hardy islanders still brave the thunderous Atlantic in their frail wooden boats, the 'currachs', still attempting to scrape a living from the barren rocks, as their forefathers did. As Brian Cleeve recounts in his excellent and pungent *A View of Ireland*, this romantic view of a lost culture was somewhat distorted some years ago, when a distinguished historian concluded that the Aran Islanders were all descended from a garrison of English soldiers quartered there by Cromwell! I'd say that you can probably give as much credence to that, as to the popular mythology about Ireland's dark haired and eyed women being descended from the remnants of the Spanish Armada washed up from their wrecked galleons on the West Coast . . . .

Brian has another interesting Cromwellian speculation. Apparently, on the day before Cromwell set the town of Drogheda, in County Louth, to fire and the sword, skewering many of its defenders on spikes along the town's walls, Drogheda's town council met to discuss the lack of streetlighting. Cool enough, you would think for a town under cruel siege. What's even more extraordinary is that the day *after* Cromwell's appalling savagery, the town council met again. And, according to the records, all they discussed once more was the streetlighting! Not a mention of rape, pillage, fire nor murder! It makes our modern accusations of governmental 'control' of information in time of war seem a little weak . . . . Or was the 'massacre' Irish propaganda . . . ?

Drogheda is on the River Boyne, where in 1690 was fought the famous battle, one of the few fought on Irish soil that had significance for the rest of Europe. At the Battle of the Boyne, Protestant forces under King William (Billy) of Orange defeated the Catholic army of James Stuart. King James lost his throne that day, and the great victory has been celebrated on the 12th of July ever since by Orangemen all over the world, but particularly in Northern Ireland. What perhaps they don't know, or would rather keep quiet about is that when the news reached Rome, Pope Innocent XI ordered a 'Te Deum' to be sung in St Peter's. At the time Catholic James was a greater thorn in the Pope's side than Protestant Billy!

This shop at Recess in Co Connemara is selling the typical selection of any Irish general store: Beer, Books, Eggs, Marble, Wool.

Mike Stead tells me that when he was taking this picture in Dingle's main street, a local fisherman had come to call and had left a fish on the stool in the doorway, and did so all the way down the street. Whether he ever got paid for the fish, we'll never know.

The owners of another shop in Dingle take great pleasure with their colour scheme.

The Olde Corner Shop in Wexford

A shop front in Crookhaven, Co Cork – but Mike didn't see Toni that day

This shop in a village near Strokestown in Co Roscommon appears to sell anything from plants to old plough seats – probably would have an Irish man-trap if you asked nicely enough.

Ireland's Unique Drink

When not cycling endlessly to school and battling with the Jesuits' earnest attempts to fill my empty head with Homer, Xenophon, and the Gaelic poems of the Fenian Cycle, I would turn the wheels of my precious little velocipede on the road to Ennis, capital of the 'Banner' County, Clare. A few miles out on the road, there stood a well-preserved fifteenth-century castle, Bunratty. It's even better preserved these days: tarted up even, for the benefit of passing tourists, who enjoy medieval banquets there, spearing

their medieval roast battery chicken with hunting knives in the approved Henry VIII/Charles Laughton fashion, downing posset-cups of foaming mead as in the days of yore, listening to sweet-voiced harpists and being left for as long as five minutes in a gen—u—wine Norman dungeon.

Close by is Durty Nelly's, where you can put yourself in touch very quickly with a more up-to-date form of Irish carousing. All it takes is a ball or two of malt, and a couple of pints of good old Arthur's black stuff, the stout. The stout is more famed in song and

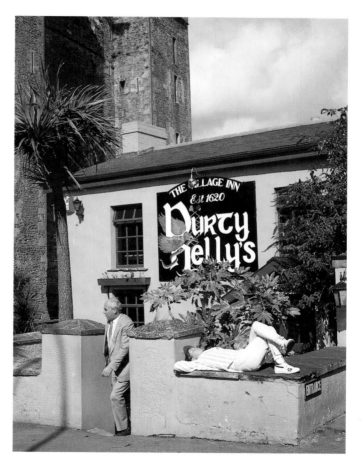

DURTY NELLY'S PUB, CO CLARE

This is certainly a more convivial place to be for a spot of Irish carousing than at the pseudo-medieval banquets held in Bunratty Castle, so loved by our tourist friends.

◁ BUNRATTY CASTLE, CO CLARE

This keep was built in the fifteenth century and is still in remarkable condition. In the nearby Folk Park, reconstructed Irish cottages and farmhouses can be visited – a great tourist attraction.

Irish stories than the whiskey. The whiskey is a kind of Scots thing, but stout, the black porter, is uniquely Irish and the Irish are extremely proud of it. They are extremely proud of how they pour it, extremely proud of what it tastes like, and extremely proud of how they can drink it. It is common knowledge in Ireland that a good pint of stout can not be got, for love nor money, outside of Ireland; indeed it is fairly common knowledge within the environment of the Pale and the Liberties of Dublin that the only decent pint of stout is to be got *there*, and nowhere else outside spitting distance of the St James' Brewery where old Arthur set up his stall in the first place. It is generally agreed that

Reminding myself of the grand taste of Irish stout, in the Powerscourt Arms Hotel.

MULLIGAN'S

Mulligan's pub in Dublin is supposed to be where you can drink the best stout in the whole of Ireland – but everyone has their favourite place, and – 'The Pint of Stout is your only man!'

outside of Ireland you'd be only wasting your time having a pint of stout, not only do they not know how to keep it, they don't know how to pour it and they don't know how to drink it. You can hardly find an Irish short story without stout in it and, if it comes to that, you can hardly find an Irishman who hasn't got stout in him. Or an Irish woman for that matter. Indeed it is quite a smart drink for the young Irish ladies these days, the black stout. Mulligan's pub in Dublin is supposed to be where you get the best stout, the best pint, but each Dublin person, each aficionado, each expert, (and *everybody* in Dublin is an expert at everything, but particularly stout), will tell you where to get the Best Pint. You could end up extremely drunk at the end of the day if you took everybody's advice, in fact you might never see home nor mother again. They do say that Dublin's sovereign brew is due to the 'regulations'. If you are a limited company, then you have to clean your pipes, (it's the way it was explained to me and I don't believe a word of it but I'm telling you and you can draw your own conclusions) – and if you're a family house, then you *don't* have to clean your pipes, and, therefore, the accumulations of centuries of gunk and unspeakable things, as well as the residue of ancient stout in the pipes, are what gave the Arthur Guinness its 'body'. There are some who would prefer the bottled stout; my father-in-law for one. I think it's for the kick, the kick inside. The old gaseous retort. The serious stout drinker, he has it down in Mulligan's and up in Neary's and he has it poured for him lovingly. It takes about five minutes and when you look at it, it's like, well, a good Irish coffee: the black body and the white smooth head. If anyone pours you a drink that is coffee-coloured, what you have there is a duff Irish coffee, and an even duffer pint of stout. It should be so well poured that the barman can inscribe a shamrock on its white head. Then you drink the black through the white and that's a Pint of Stout. Accept no substitutes. The Irish are as pernickety about their stout as the London clubman is about his port, or the Yuppie about his claret. Arthur Guinness and his stout spawned so many lords and ladies, and indeed, cabinet ministers in Britain, that it must be good stuff.

When I was a growing boy, if you didn't become a banker or an insurance clerk, or if your father wasn't a doctor, a quantity surveyor or an architect, and you were particularly bright, you went for a job in the Civil Service, or a Clerkship at Arthur Guinness of the First Class. Clerkship at Guinness' was regarded as a damn good thing, a Bobby's Job, and it was rumoured that you got a *free* pint of stout with your lunch, incentive enough for most people. I had a job near Arthur Guinness & Son once, indeed my first job, with the Royal Bank of Ireland up at Corn Market, the most historical part of Dublin. Up there, near the Liberties, near where Dean Swift had his church, near Christchurch, was as close as I ever got. I wasn't quite bright enough for the Civil Service, and certainly not for a Clerkship of the First Class up at St James' Gate. My father wanted me to be a doctor but I couldn't see myself hammering away at the books for seven years and anyway, the Jesuits in their wisdom, had educated us, the Honours Boys, the 'A' stream in modern parlance, in the Classics. The Pass stream did chemistry and applied maths and the sciences. It meant, of course, that all the lads who were really bright enough to become doctors knew absolutely nothing by the time they came to their first year in Medical School, and had to work like stink to get their chemistry; so I wouldn't have got that anyway. With no job in the offing, I went back to Belvedere College and studied philosophy. Belvedere was in Great Denmark Street; a street of once imposing Georgian houses, most of which were being allowed to slip into decay. It used to be the best part of Dublin, but in the 40s and 50s the north side of Dublin seemed to go into a decline.

THE ROYAL BANK OF IRELAND

This was my first office – not bad for a start. You'd think the least they could have done was put up a plaque! Maybe they're preserving it for the nation . . . .

Dublin II

Discipline at Belvedere was a doddle compared with the Dothe Boys Hall atmosphere I'd had to endure at Crescent College in Limerick. They were far too gentle for me – I never learnt a thing. They played cricket in Belvedere but I could never master that; I came too late to reach any standard and it terrified me – people hurling an extremely hard ball at me at about eighty miles an hour was not something that I thought one should do for fun and I thought the whole thing a great deal more dangerous than rugby. I played in the rugby team in Belvedere. My great love, tennis, I was unable to pursue, because the tennis courts for the school were simply too far away even for me and my little bicycle to master. I would cycle to school every day, as in the time honoured days of Limerick, but I didn't come home for lunch, it was that little bit too far. We're talking Big Town here.

Belvedere was where James Joyce was educated, before his father sent him off to the more rigorous Clongowes in County Meath, a boarding school that as I've said elsewhere, really belongs to my family. I've been to Clongowes once, to play rugby there, and I know exactly why James Joyce wasn't all that keen on it – it was the coldest place I was ever in, in my life. Wormwood Scrubs would have been snug in comparison, but then, I was always a bit of a mammy's boy. James Joyce wasn't all that keen on Belvedere either and Belvedere was certainly not keen on James Joyce. We weren't encouraged to read the great man, indeed, we weren't encouraged to *mention* him – he'd let the side down . . . .

I read philosophy with a German tutor, a dear man who always said to us, 'Remember, boys, you will never think the same again, after you've done philosophy' and he was right – I've been confused ever since. We philosophers were a select band, sitting at the backs of classes, deep in Descartes, and swanning around like gentlemen. There were three of us. We would take coffee and then, in between classes, would stroll in a gentlemanly manner, down O'Connell Street, broad and suave. The Irish like to think that O'Connell Street is the broadest boulevard in Europe – I'm not sure they are right, but the Irish tend to do a bit of talking like that from time to time; they don't necessarily want you to believe it but they still like to say things like 'the grass is greener in Ireland than anywhere else' – this is usually said by somebody who has never been outside the parish in his life.

O'CONNELL STREET IN DUBLIN

The Irish like to think it is the broadest and the best boulevard in Europe. You'd be as well not to mention Paris. That kind of showing off is not appreciated . . . .

DUBLIN

My Granny always referred to the place as 'Dear Old Dirty Dublin', but lest you forget, this was once 'the second city of the British Empire'. It celebrates its Millenium this year, but already some smart-alecs are saying they've got the date wrong, and it should be next year. There's no pleasing some people . . . .

The mighty emporium of Clerys in O'Connell Street where Auntie Nellie used to work

O'Connell Bridge, over the Liffey. Incidentally, the Lord Mayor of Dublin, Carmencita Hederman, tells me that Dublin is now one of Europe's cleanest capitals. 'Dear old clean Dublin' doesn't have the same ring, does it . . . ?

Inspecting the purity of the Liffey – and deciding it was much improved

We philosophers would stroll down O'Connell Street, taking in the sights, admiring the ladies and daring to go into the Gresham Hotel to use the loo. It was a lovely city, Dublin, and the sun seemed to shine a lot. It didn't seem quite as damp as Limerick; down one side of O'Connell Street we would go, passing the mighty emporium of Clery's, where my Aunt Nellie worked, and then, over O'Connell Bridge. You could smell O'Connell Bridge before you got to it; mainly because the Liffey was running underneath it. The Liffey, Anna Livia Plurabelle, a small but dynamic river, carried most of Dublin's sewage to the sea. It always struck me as extraordinarily plucky of the people who used to participate every year for charity in what was called 'the Liffey Swim'. The great Dublin wit, Oliver St John Gogarty, once swam across the Liffey to avoid his pursuers, and when somebody said to him, 'I believe you swam the Liffey,' he said, 'No, I was just going through the motions!'

Across the Liffey then, O'Connell Bridge with its statue of Daniel O'Connell, the Liberator. Somewhere, around about the 50s, some bright spark in the Irish Civil Service or Tourist Board decided that 'Ireland was a Festival' and that Ireland was going to be a Festival in April, probably its rainiest month. It was to be called 'AN/TOSTAL – the Festival'. It didn't seem to attract a lot of tourists. It didn't seem to attract a great deal of enthusiasm from the locals either. There were a lot of what can only be described as excesses done in the name of 'AN/TOSTAL'. The major excess was a thing called the 'Bowl of Light' which some idiot placed in the middle of the broad expanse of O'Connell Bridge – a plastic number, it was, a large bowl of plastic flames that glimmered day and night. Lovely. One night, some gentleman, overcome by sensitivity, or perhaps drink, picked up the Bowl of Light, and threw it into the Liffey, never to be seen again. It marked the end of 'AN/TOSTAL', but I don't think many people noticed it.

The Grand Union Canal, Dublin

Festivals

Ireland has never been short of Festivals – any excuse for a hooley . . . . There are Folk Festivals the length and breadth of the country, with singers, dancers and instrumentalists taking over whole towns, for as long as a week, with competitions and medals to be won for fiddlers, four-hand reels, pipe-playing and any other musical activity you can shake a leg at. There's Puck Fair, in Killorglin, County Kerry, where every year the tinkers, the travelling people, foregather for a week of roistering, fighting, horse-trading, singing and general diversion. What perhaps singles this particular festival out from the myriad of others, is its blatantly pagan centrepiece – a large billy-goat, placed on a high platform, festooned in flowers and treated as an idol for the week! How this tradition has survived in Holy Catholic Ireland, for all those years, remains a mystery.

The Galway Oyster Festival is still going strong, as good an excuse as any for downing copious draughts of Guinness along with the bi-valved mollusc that gives the festival its name. If, after a couple of dozen, you couldn't care if you never saw another oyster again till the end of your days, there's tons of good Irish smoked salmon, and yards of home-made bread, the like of which you'll find nowhere else. There are competitions here too, for the World's Best Oyster-Opener, and many people I know have set their own Personal Best marks here, mainly in the competitive Pint of Stout field. Some, I know, have never really recovered, and go from one Oyster Festival to the next, not very sure where they've been in the intervening twelve months . . . .

The same was true of the Kilkenny Beer Festival, which I hope continues to thrive. Kilkenny itself is an impressive historic town with an imposing castle. It was here in 1366 that the 'Statutes of Kilkenny' attempted to stop Norman/Irish intermarriage, and the assimilation of the Normans into a Gaelic culture, and in 1642, an Irish General Assembly was formed to try and keep English hands off Irish land. With the usual results. . . . All a far cry from the good old Beer Festival, where I spent many a happy night celebrating Kilkenny's worthy cause. One memorable year, carloads of Ireland's new television stars descended on Kilkenny, as an added attraction to the beer. We played a charity football match, which was as near to utter chaos as I ever hope to get, and then got tarted up for a grand dinner and ball. I remember little of the food or dancing, probably because the place was awash with the aforementioned object of the enterprise, but I have a clear recall of a somewhat inebriated female taking my wife aside on several occasions, and saying loudly and deliberately, 'You are a *lady*, Helen, a *lady*!' I'm sure no slur was intended, but I've always taken it as a soft impeachment and resented the unspoken implication that it was a crying shame that a 'lady' couldn't find someone a bit more suitable than yours truly.

Let me not forget either the prestigious Wexford Opera Festival, a remarkable yearly musical triumph for that lovely harbour town on the very south-east tip of the country, which attracts an international array of artistes and music lovers, has premiered so many important operas, and revived many a jaded musical palate.

The Dublin Theatre Festival flourishes apace, and so too, the Festival of Italian Opera staged by the Dublin Grand Opera Society. I'm proud to say that I played an active part in some of those Italian operas. In an attempt to get in for nothing, a pal and myself offered our services as 'supers', or extras. I've been a Venetian bystander while the drama of *Otello* has unfolded, a passing priest while the magnificent 'Easter Hymn' from *Cavalleria Rusticana* has been sung, an Assyrian slave in *Aida*, and a waiter in *La Traviata*. It wasn't plain sailing, mind you. I got into the operas for nothing, but things got a bit fraught. For instance, the Italian producer didn't seem all that keen on my performance in *La Traviata*. Possibly he felt that suede shoes were not quite the thing for waiters in the nineteenth century. Nit-picking, I call it. My friend and I refused to smear our pale bodies with the cocoa butter required, apparently, to simulate the general appearance of an Assyrian. We must have seemed the two most consumptive-looking slaves ever seen in *Aida*.

However, my most memorable night was good old *Cavalleria*. As in every theatre, the Green Room was the place where everyone congregated, for a refreshing beverage or several. Actors and singers rarely partake before or during a performance, but we extras felt the need to keep our strength up for our exacting performance, viz; walking solemnly round the stage during the Easter procession. Talk was racy that night, with one word borrowing another, and the time slipped by while the drinks slipped down. Someone had just ordered another round, one of the altar boys, I think, when the producer came storming into the Green Room. 'Ah!' he shouted in typical over-excited Italian fashion, 'You like to drank you beer? Drink!! The procession, she is over! You can go at home!' We slunk from the Green Room, never to grace the stage of the Dublin Grand Opera Society again . . . . You know, I *still* wonder what that great 'Easter Hymn' processional must have looked like from the circle, without altar boys, priests, bishops or nuns. Were the audience so engrossed that they never noticed?

Opera audiences *do* have to suspend disbelief quite severely. One night in *Il Travatore*, I watched, fascinated, as a gypsy stuck his knife into a table, dragged it out again, and stabbed a rival viciously to death, singing the while. Unfortunately, he'd jammed the knife so far into the table that the handle came away. Our hero, without a falter had hacked his rival viciously to death with the handle. Everybody in the audience saw it. Not a giggle. Nary a titter. Probably afraid people would think they weren't 'serious' opera-goers. It wasn't like that in the old days, according to the Da'. He used to frequent the 'gods' for many an operatic evening, in the days of his grocer's apprenticeship, and he recalled the Dublin audience of those days as being far less inhibited in their attitude. Downright noisy, was how my father described them; quick to cheer, even quicker to jeer, but always fair-minded if a chap had done his best. My father remembered one occasion, when a tenor had attacked his aria with great gusto, but not much finesse. Muted applause greeted the end of the aria, and over it, from the 'gods', the encouraging word: 'A brave effort, me son. A brave effort . . . . '

Dublin III

Walking gently on, over O'Connell Bridge, through the mass of cyclists, one could pick out the Ballast Office; and the Ballast Office Clock, which James Joyce referred to as an 'epiphany' – I've never really understood that, I must ask Frank Delaney. We philosophers would stroll on gently, to the Bank of Ireland, an imposing colonnade, which was once the Irish Houses of Parliament, and on the left, the grand buildings of Trinity College. Trinity College, at least when I was about, was a place for Protestants; the Archbishop of Dublin had declared that no Catholic could go there to complete his studies or pass his degree. It was, and remains, an outstanding university, second only, historically, to Oxford and Cambridge. However, to the Irish it had been a bastion of English supremacy for years and also a hotbed of what could only be described as liberality, and, probably, s–e–x. The Archbishop of Dublin, a somewhat conservative man, felt that the good Irish Catholic boy and girl would be better off up at University

TRINITY COLLEGE, DUBLIN

At one time, the Archbishop of Dublin would only allow Protestants to attend the college, the Catholics going to University College, Dublin. But all that's changed now; it would scarcely matter if you were a member of Islamic Jihad . . . .

BEWLEY'S IN DUBLIN

Here the smell of coffee would knock you down as you walked past. And it is still a great place for a genteel dish.

College, Dublin – the Catholic university, than be having his morals and general behaviour besmirched by association with the Protestants and English people at Trinity College, Dublin.

Trinity College houses perhaps Ireland's greatest treasure, the eighth-century Book of Kells, which any visitor to Ireland should see. It is probably the finest example of an illustrated manuscript; the Gospels written in Latin, with an unbelievable profusion of illustrative detail – letters, pictures, birds, animals, all done in convoluted, intricate detail and meticulous colour. Heaven knows how long it took to produce this flowering of devotion and artistry, but it is the outstanding product of a period when Ireland provided the single light of hope in the tunnel of the Dark Ages.

Swinging round by the Bank of Ireland, we'd walk down the other side of D'Olier Street, passing Bewley's, where the smell of coffee would knock you down. I couldn't afford a coffee in those days, because I was a penniless philosopher, but later on, as a member of the banking fraternity, and indeed a boy broadcaster, I would often cross the bridge with friends and drop in at Bewley's, lured by the extraordinary smell of newly-ground coffee. The coffee was so strong at Bewley's that after a couple of cups, you'd walk back across the bridge with your feet three feet off the ground and a headache that would last you for about four days. I used to drop into Bewley's for a cup of reviving brew with the bank's porter, when I worked at Phibsborough in Dublin. As Junior Boy at Phibsborough, the bank manager, in his wisdom, would entrust me and the porter with £5,000 in used notes. It was our job to carry these, fresh-faced and fine-featured, in an unmarked bag, on the bus, to the Head Office of the Royal Bank of Ireland, where we would smartly take it inside and have it exchanged; the old notes for new ones. Then, placed in the same unmarked bag, the money would be carried back by myself and the porter to the Royal Bank of Ireland, Phibsborough. On reflection, and

THE FOUR COURTS IN DUBLIN

OVERLEAF AND BELOW *The Four Courts were built in 1802 and almost completely destroyed in the Civil War of 1921.*

indeed at the time, it seemed a somewhat foolhardy enterprise, because £5,000 was not an amount to be laughed at in those days; not many would chuckle at it now. The sheer foolishness of it, astonishes me even yet. The bank porter and I would sit in Bewley's imbibing strong draughts of coffee and he would tell me what to do in the event of a wrong-doer or rapscallion attempting to grab hold of our £5,000 in new notes. The answer was simple – hand it over. We were not being paid to give our young lives up for the benefit of the bank, was how the porter put it, and he was no chicken.

In fact the porter was a Scot, with a German name, who lived in a house painted fire-engine red. He was a spoiled music-hall performer, who could often be heard doing instrumental impressions in the safe. His trumpet was uncanny, with or without mute, and his banjo was okay too. He had a dream. He could see it all: a great theatre, the curtain down. Then, from behind the curtain, the sound of a great orchestra playing Basie, or even Beethoven. The curtain slowly rises – and lo and behold! – the 'orchestra' is seen to be a hundred instrumental impressionists: I thought it might get boring after a couple of encores, but the porter was convinced he was on to a winner. He was only marking time in the bank until he could gather his fellow-impressionists together. The porter's union couldn't have been all that hot on job description, because as well as risking his life for the bank, he was also required to cook the manager's lunch. It was a good job the manager never saw the porter kick his chop around the floor before he cooked it. . . .

Sated with coffee and the odd sticky bun, back we'd go, the porter and me, on the bus with our new notes, over O'Connell Bridge. Down one side of the quays, The Four Courts, an impressive building which got knocked about a bit in the Civil War, but has been restored to its glory, and then the lovely little Ha'penny Bridge – so called because that was the toll to cross the Liffey there. On the other side of the O'Connell Bridge, looking towards the Estuary, a not so pretty bridge – an eyesore of a railway bridge, part of Dublin's Loop-Line, which further compounds its ugliness by obscuring the view of Dublin's finest building, James Gandon's Custom House – beautiful in stone, green dome, clock; what a pity you can't see it from O'Connell Bridge, but it's certainly worth a walk down the quays to have a look. On then along O'Connell Street, past the O'Connell Monument of the Great Liberator, and at the far end of the mighty boulevard, another monument, to yet another great man in Irish history – Parnell, who went even closer than O'Connell in the pursuance of the dream of Irish unity, but whose hopes were dashed by a foolish dalliance with a woman, for which neither his Parliamentary opponents, nor the Irish Catholic Church, ever forgave him. In the middle of O'Connell Street, facing where the much maligned and much missed Nelson's Pillar, used to be, is probably Ireland's greatest historic monument. The GPO, where, in 1916, a few brave, some would say foolhardy Volunteers, against the might of the British Army, declared an Irish Republic. The declaration of that Republic is still to be seen on a plaque within the GPO by the statue of Ireland's greatest mythological hero, Cuchulainn. It was here that Padraig Pearse and his fellow Volunteers fought for several days, before being finally overwhelmed and taken away to their execution. That very execution, which according to W.B. Yeats, gave birth to 'a terrible beauty'. Many an IRA pension has

The Ha'penny Bridge

This is a lovely little bridge which crosses the Liffey – for pedestrians only. It was once a toll bridge. Guess what you had to pay?

been paid out on the basis of heroic service in the GPO during the Uprising of 1916, and it is not unknown to hear it said, that if all the people that were drawing a pension because of service in 1916 got together, the queue would stretch several times around the GPO . . . .

I was lucky, as a boy broadcaster, to be given the task of commentating on the celebrations to mark the Fiftieth Anniversary of the Easter Uprising, to describe the

THE GENERAL POST OFFICE IN DUBLIN

Probably Ireland's greatest historical monument, this was the scene of the 1916 Easter Uprising. The recently erected statue commemorates Jim Larkin, the famous labour leader, who is depicted in a typical pose.

colourful scene as the might of Ireland's Armed Forces marched proudly past the GPO, and its reviewing stand. It was my solemn task to describe all that happened, in copious detail, including the dignitaries that were gathered for this auspicious and historic event. I set myself and my microphone up, and got ready to let loose a barrage of pith and moment. Unfortunately, as the Boys in Green marched by the great facade, I realised all too readily, that whilst I could tell who was marching past, I could not say who they were marching past, if you're still with me. Some bright spark had forgotten to send out the invitations to the dignitaries that were supposed to assemble in the reviewing stand; so there I was with a list of famous names, as long as your arm, and not a one in sight, while in the reviewing stand were gathered a selection of Dublin's hooligans, urchins and some tourists, who happened to be passing and were pressed into service by the officials. I suppose it prepared me for the worst excesses of British Broadcasting. As a matter of fact, when I actually started in Irish Radio, we were based in the GPO; and that is where my earliest recollections of broadcasting begin – the setting fire to fellow announcers' scripts . . . the pouring of water over their heads even as they broadcast, the removal of traditional fiddlers' boots as they played, because the thumping was drowning the music . . . .

Being trapped in the lift with three members of the *Dáil*, during a General Election broadcast. . . . Playing a record entitled 'Isn't It Grand Boys to be Bloody Well Dead' on a *hospitals* request programme . . . ad libbing masterfully, when a record gets stuck in a groove: 'Ah, I appear to have got stuck in the middle of 'The Spanish Lady' ' . . . taking over a live quiz show on television without knowing the rules, while the production team forget the prizes . . . the guitarist who fell off her stool even as I introduced her . . . the handing over to a reporter for an outside broadcast, to be met with silence on three occasions, then, on the fourth all-or-nothing try, to hear, 'Sorry. This is the engineer, Mick's not here at the moment' . . . listening to a two-way link-up between Sydney and Dublin, where following an Olivia Newton-John record, the lady announcer in Dublin says, 'That was one of your Australian compatriots, Olivia Newton-John – what do you think of her?' Australian voice: 'Well, she's got good legs!' Irish lady announcer: 'No, but legs apart, what do you think of her? . . . .' Oh, memories, memories . . . .

Down there on the other side of the Street, one of Ireland's grandest hotels, the Gresham. It was here that Irish television celebrated its opening night with a grand *soirée*. It was snowing outside, but inside the Gresham all was glitter, all was glamour, all was on a wing and a prayer. If just one little plug had come out of its socket that was the end of this outside broadcast; but it all worked perfectly, and with that splendid lack of sense of occasion to which I have already referred – the jeering of Presidents at football matches, the booing at O'Casey Plays at the Abbey, the Dublin jackeens lowered themselves to the occasion once again. Even as the No. 1 Army Band attempted to play, and the tenor attempted to serenade us, the snowballs flew in all directions from the jeering gurriers who couldn't have cared less whether Irish television opened or closed. Snowballs disappeared down the bassoons and euphoniums, hit the singer on the back of the head, knocked over music stands, and rendered the conductor semi-conscious. Very few television services could have opened in such auspicious style . . . .

IRELAND'S WILDLIFE

Ireland is the land of the horse, of course, but one mustn't forget the humble donkey which still carries the creels of turf from the bog. Neddy is still a beast of burden all over Ireland.

Donkeys in Co Cork

Horses in Co Tipperary

The donkey wagon in Ballyduff, Co Limerick

'Have you heard the latest Irish joke?'

Tinkers are a familiar sight all over Ireland.

Joseph Dunne, a busker, performing in Limerick

Young buskers in Dublin

Blarney Castle and Cork

The Dubliner speaks through his nose, rather like a Liverpudlian; it must be something to do with the proximity to the sea, or possibly, holding the aforesaid proboscis every time he has to cross the Liffey.

In Cork, on the other hand, people talk in a light sing-song way, which others mock. 'Are 'oo from Cork? I am, are 'oo? D'you ate potatoes? Bedad, I'do. . . .'

I remember driving down through Tipperary with a friend, and as we crossed the County border into Cork, he rolled down the window and breathed deeply: 'Do you smell the shrewd air?' Cork people are famed in song and story, and no little feared, for their shrewdness. They are, of course, the same as all other Irish people except that Cork has always been a prosperous port. It is in Cork that you'll find the Blarney stone, and you

Blarney Castle, Co Cork

The Irish are reputed always to kiss the Blarney Stone which is then supposed to impart the gift of the gab. I've never met an Irishman who'd go within a mile of the place . . . .

can hang by your ankles and kiss this lump of rock at the top of Blarney Castle. The Irish are always reputed to have kissed the Blarney stone; it is something no self-respecting Irishman would ever do. The idea of hanging by your ankles to kiss a bit of stone is not something that is uppermost in any Irishman's ambitions, although doubtless thousands, nay millions of tourists have done it, and continue to do so every year on the off-chance that it will bequeath them the gift of the gab.

As Dublin is on the Liffey, and Limerick is on the Shannon, so Cork sits astride the

<u>Cork</u>

Cork sits astride the River Lee – literally, since Ireland's second largest city was built on the banks of the river and the surrounding marshes.

St Finbar's Cathedral was built in the French Gothic style between 1865 and 1880.

River Lee. 'The banks of my own Lovely Lee', and the bells of Shandon can be heard in Cork city. As the Bow Bells ring in London for the true Cockney, so the true Corkonian is born within the sound of the Shandon Bells.

Cork, like every other town, and most people, has its peculiarities. I was there a few years ago, with a couple of BBC friends, for the opening of the second Irish television channel, RTE2. As we drove from the opening, on a rainswept night, my two friends were astounded at the number of people walking up and down Patrick Street, which is Cork's main thoroughfare. It was 11 o'clock, the rain was coming down in bucketfulls and there were these people, walking up and down. I had to explain that they were doing 'Panna' – don't ask me where the word derives from; but in the same way that the Spaniards of Barcelona on a balmy evening, parade the Ramblas – girls at one side, boys the other, eyeing each other, so the people of Cork, in considerably less clement conditions, walk up and down Patrick Street.

In County Cork, there is now the famous village of Ballinspittle, where between 1986 and 1987 the miracle of the 'moving statues' first came to light. It caused a tremendous upsurge of religious revival in Ireland and a certain amount of scepticism elsewhere. Apparently, the statue of the Virgin Mary, on the roadside near Ballinspittle, had moved. Not far, just a smidgin. From all over Ireland, and from further afield too, thousands of people, mostly women, flocked with their rosary beads to pray to the moving statue. Very soon, Ballinspittle became a commercial hub, and in a trice, other moving statues were spotted in various parts of the country. Apparently, the one man, the one statue maker, made them all. He himself, when questioned closely, said that he had had several of these statues back into the foundry for repair from time to time and closely as he had watched them, not one of them had ever shimmered. With their usual mix of sentimentality, faith and cynicism, the Irish could not resist the joke. There is a statue of Master McGrath, the legendary Irish greyhound in Kildare, I think; apparently that had been arrested, for worrying the sheep. Another tale was told of the blessed Virgin being knocked down by a lorry in Mount Mellick as she tried to cross the road on a corner . . . . Ballinspittle has gone very quiet recently, but the people of Ireland have always had a great faith and trust in the Blessed Virgin and in God and although many observers would be inclined to say that if you look at the most immobile object for long enough, it will appear to move just a little and the more so if the other people around are, perhaps, in a somewhat overwrought state. But who is to deny these people their faith and their belief?

Patrick Street. Ireland is a country which is famed in song and story for its predilection to drink but, at the same time, nowhere would you find so many statues to the great prohibitionist, Father Mathew. He started a movement, later called the Pioneers, round about 1838; the movement gained enormous ground in Ireland in the 1930s, 40s, 50s. It required its members to eschew all drink forever, and wear a little badge which showed they were part of the movement. I used to be a Pioneer – but then as my father always said: 'Many are called – but few get up . . . .'

Kinsale and Bantry Bay

THE CHARLES FORT

This stands in the attractive village of Summercove near Kinsale and was built between 1670 and 1677. It is a very well-preserved example of a star fort.

KINSALE, CO CORK ▷

Kinsale and its harbour look just like an English harbour town for the simple reason that it was built by the English, as were the two forts which stand either side of the mouth of the harbour.

THE HEAD OF KINSALE

Off this headland, in 1915, the Cunard liner Lusitania *was sunk by a German U-boat. The tragedy is commemorated by a memorial in Cobh, near Cork, where there is also a museum featuring the disaster.*

Outside Cork is the lovely little port and harbour of Kinsale, where in 1601 a force of Spaniards landed unopposed to free Ireland from the thrall of Elizabeth's Protestant England. They were to be joined by the Ulster Chieftains, the O'Neills and O'Donnells. Unfortunately, O'Neill and O'Donnell were defeated by the English General, Mountjoy, just outside Kinsale. Some say that battle was the beginning of the end of Gaelic Ireland.

The Lusitania Memorial, Cobh

Kinsale is still there, as lovely as ever, like a little English harbour town, with houses spilling down towards the sea, and it's full of good restaurants. Kinsale is a great centre for fishing. I did a documentary there once, for Irish television, which required me to go out and catch a shark, which indeed I did, on a storm-tossed sea. They threw the revolting 'rubby-dubby' which is the entrails of other fish and smells like the wrath of God, into the sea, which attracted the shark, and I caught him. It was supposed to be recorded for posterity, but unfortunately the cameraman, who was in the well of the boat, was being as sick as a parrot throughout this momentous piscatorial triumph. I suppose you won't believe I caught a shark, either?

The last time I visited Kinsale was with my two friends from the BBC. I wanted them to

BANTRY BAY, CO CORK

ABOVE *Another one of Mike's photos that gives the game away about Irish weather. Let's call it 'changeable', a favourite Irish euphemism. Just as 'a soft day' means that you can't see your hand in front of your face for the rain. I remember a country-woman saying to me once: 'Sure, that sort of rain wouldn't wet you.' And meaning it . . . .*

RIGHT *Boats – little and luxurious – on Bantry Bay*

EVENING ENTERTAINMENT IN
BANTRY

I'm not sure if the Parish Priest would have allowed this class of thing in the good old days . . . .

see the place in all its beauty. It was off-season, so most of the restaurants were closed, but we found a pub that was open. As we walked in, I spied the chef playing billiards. Someone asked if we'd like anything to eat. We said 'why not?' and the chef put down his billiard cue and went off and brought us back some of the most delicious curried prawns I've ever had in my life. Then the proprietor arrived and it began to rain Irish coffee, and as we staggered out of the place in the wee small hours, a man sitting at the bar, in a Saville Row suit, accosted me. In well-modulated English tones he said, 'Hello, you're Terry Wogan, aren't you?' I was amazed at the recognition. I don't know how long he'd been sitting at the bar; he's probably still there – just another example of an Englishman who had come across for a weekend and got lost in the Celtic mists . . . .

It's easy in Cork, as it is anywhere in Ireland, to be bewitched by the scenery: of Bantry Bay, or down in Glengarrif where palm trees and tropical plants grow in profusion, and strange creatures are occasionally found washed up on the shore, because that particular corner of Ireland gets the full brunt of the Gulf Stream – it has travelled beneath the ocean all the way from the Caribbean, and is responsible for the 'mild' Irish climate, mild being a euphemism for a climate which even in summer, strikes an uneasy balance between sunshine and showers.

View from a ruined cottage near Sneem, looking across the Kenmare estuary to the Beara Peninsula

The Kerry Coast and the Dingle Peninsula

Just as the English tell Irish jokes, and indeed, the Dutch tell Belgian jokes, and for all I know, the Spanish tell Portuguese jokes, so the Irish tell Kerryman jokes. The Kerryman is supposed to be, well, to put it kindly, a little on the 'thick' side. This, of course, is no more true than saying that the Cork man is a damn sight shrewder than any other sort of Irishman. You won't put one over on a Kerryman all that quickly, let me tell you. Kerry is a county of a staggering beauty, again with the Gulf Stream gently in and out of its many bays. I spent a marvellous holiday with my family, years and years ago, when God was a boy, down near the peninsula of Inch, on Dingle Bay in Kerry. We stayed there in a house that belonged to Mary-Ann. The facilities weren't all that good – if you wished to attend to your ablutions, the place to do it was a good way away from the house, behind a bush. We rode donkeys, seemed to eat an awful lot of stew, ran around barefoot amongst the chickens and the hens and one day, I took a trip on Mary-Ann's side car to Anascaul – the nearest village. I fell off the side-car trying to be smart and had a bump the size of a duck egg on my head for the remainder of the holiday. The things you remember . . . .

Tralee is the capital town of the county of Kerry, the subject of a song called 'The Rose of Tralee'. Someone, in the Tralee Town Council or Board of Tourist Management, decided it would be a good idea to pick an international 'Rose of Tralee', and so, from all four corners of the earth were culled glamorous ladies of the most tenuous Irish, let alone Tralee, connections, flown in to Shannon airport, and bedecked with flowers. There were Roses of Tralee from Bogota, from Caracas, from Turkey, from Korea, and they asked me to compère it, and for several years I did. My wife came down with me; walking down the street, minding her own business, wearing slacks, a little urchin ran up to her and said, 'Give us a penny, will you ma'am?' Rather brusquely she said, 'No, off with you.' She'd only gone a few yards when he shouted, 'And will you look at the big backside on her anyway.' On another occasion, the present Mrs Wogan accompanied the Ladies' Committee for a dish of tea and cucumber sandwich. There was dancing and merriment, and a bold youth came up to my wife, and said, 'Well Miss, would you like to dance.' I don't know how it is now, but certainly, when I was in my teens and twenties, a lady simply did not refuse. If you were asked to dance, you did, and you suffered the bad breath, the smell of the stale stout, the pimples and the groping. It was not the ladies' place to say 'no' – it was the ladies' place to refuse to walk home with the gentleman afterwards, but the least you could do for the poor eejit was to give him a dance. My wife did the unforgivable: she said, 'No'. Our hero had the answer: 'Ah, well, you're too old for me anyway . . . .'

THE SOUTH-WEST OF CORK

Take a look at all this. I spent twenty-eight years of my life in Ireland, and from the look of these pictures, I missed nearly all the best bits. So there's no need for you to be depressed if you've already been to the Island of Saints and Scholars and not taken in these stunning sights and scenes. You'll just have to go again. So will I. Ballydehob and Bantry, Roaring Water Bay (what a name!) and Skibbereen . . . .

BALLYDEHOB

This village at the top of Roaring Water Bay used to be a centre for copper mining, but the industry is now abandoned.

This castle stands sentinel on Roaring Water Bay.

Barley Cove

Barley Cove has become very fashionable which isn't surprising since it has a superb sandy beach; Brown Head can be seen beyond.

Castletownend

Near Ballydehob, this little village was where The Recollections of an Irish RM *was written.*

Mizen Head

This is the most south-westerly tip of Ireland; the cliffs are nearly 700 feet high.

OVERLEAF *Three Castle Head bathed in an Atlantic sunset*

SKIBBEREEN

The local newspaper which was called The Eagle *(I'm not sure if it is still being printed) proclaimed just before the First World War with a vast headline: THE SKIBBEREEN EAGLE HAS ITS EYE ON THE TSAR. It's probably true that what Skibbereen thinks today, the rest of the world thinks tomorrow . . . . They know a thing or two, Cork people . . . .*

THE BEARA PENINSULA

Gougane Beara (pronounced 'Googawn Barra') with its monastic site and forest park, is the entrance to the enchanting Beara Peninsula, between Bantry Bay and the Kenmare River. There's Tim Healy Pass in the Caha Mountains, Hungry Hill and Slieve Miskish, Castletownbere, Cod's Head and all these lovely places besides. Our photographer, a Lakeland Yorkshireman, admits to having lost his heart to Ireland. Somehow, I knew he would . . . .

OVERLEAF *Looking across the Kenmare River to the Beara Peninsula*

The Tim Healy Pass, and Glanmore Lake

GLENGARRIFF

The town lies in a deep lonely valley and these incredibly scarred mountains rear up behind, back to back with the Caha Mountains.

BARLEY LAKE

Barley Lake is a mountain lake and can be reached by a hazardous drive up a rough track – and a petrifying return journey.

The Coast of Kerry

This bit of the Kerry Coast is known to all visitors – especially those from overseas – as the Ring of Kerry. I doubt many Irish people actually 'do the drive'. The coastline is magnificent, especially at the Western tip.

The Slieve Miskish Mountains

That pool isn't just an ordinary watering hole but a flooded mine shaft and very deep. Not one to paddle in.

Sneem

Sneem is an attractive little place on an inlet of the Kenmare river estuary. It's pronounced 'Shneem', but they won't take offence if you get it wrong.

THE STAIGUE FORT

This is considered to be Ireland's most impressive ancient stone fort. The massive staircase within its walls can be seen in this photograph.

DERRYNANE BAY

This is on Kerry's south-western tip and has views across to the Beara Peninsula. This photograph accentuates the local rock formation, and the little stone-walled fields.

The raging Atlantic off the Kerry coast where rocks are a major hazard even to local shipping and fishermen.

Valentia Island

Valentia Island is connected to the mainland by a bridge from Portmagee. It was the starting point for the TransAtlantic telephone cable when it was laid in 1886.

The Skelligs Islands

Lying in the Atlantic off the final tip of the mainland, the two main islands are Great Skellig and Skellig Michael. The latter is cone-shaped and rises sharply to 700 feet; on the top is an amazing assortment of 10th-century buildings – two churches, two oratories and some clochans, or beehive-shaped cells used by the early monks in retreat. Rough steps hewn out of the rock are the only method of ascent, but the rocky island is now closed to the public and has been made a major bird sanctuary.

A lonely cottage on Ballinskelligs Bay near Waterville

Portmagee and the road bridge across to Valentia Island.

Carhan House, now ruined, is where the 'Liberator', the great Daniel O'Connell, was born in 1775.

BELOW *Knightstown on Valentia Island*

THE DINGLE PENINSULA

My memories of the Dingle Peninsula (in Gaelic An Daingean*) are mostly of sunny boyhood holidays spent near Annascaul. Though I remember, in later years, eating the best lobster I ever ate, in Dingle town. I remember too, a very old Kerryman telling me his memories of looking across the bay and seeing the lighted torches of the Fenians as they marched through Glenbeigh. The historic Gallerus Oratory is on the Peninsula, and from Dunquin at its very tip you can see the Blaskets.*

THE CONNOR PASS

The road from Tralee runs along the north coast overlooking Tralee Bay before crossing the peninsula on the road called the Connor Pass. The landscape is beautiful yet deserted apart from a few four-leggeds. As everywhere in Ireland, there's plenty of water to be seen in the Connor Pass. Despite the heartfelt cries that go up all over the country at opening time, no Irishman ever died of thirst . . . .

VENTRY BAY

This beautiful bay is on the way to Slea Head. The little stone-walled fields behind this tiny settlement are very Celtic in character, and are similar to ones found in some of the Yorkshire Dales.

DINGLE

This is considered to be the most westerly town in Europe. Its little harbour nestles in an inlet, and the town has a wealth of historical connections.

Slea Head

LEFT *Slea Head is the most westerly tip of the peninsula and has wonderful views across to the Blasket Islands.*

Brandon Mount

RIGHT *This is 3127 feet high and is a very popular mountain for climbing.*

The Blasket Islands ▷

These islands have been the source of some very fine writing, particularly in the mother tongue; they can be visited by boat from either Coumeenoole or Dunquin.

Dunquin

LEFT *This harbour became immediately famous when the film of* Ryan's Daughter *was released. Another claim – that Dunquin is the most westerly place in Europe to be habited.*

RIGHT *As the road turns north and then turns inland, Sibyl Point can be seen across Sibyl Bay.*

ABOVE *Still going west, towards Slea Head, one reaches Fahan, a fascinating site containing some 400 clochans, ancient beehive-style huts.*

TRALEE

The traditional end of circumnavigating the Dingle Peninsula is to return to Tralee and you will pass the windmill at Blennerville on your way in.

Tralee is like an English market town, with big wide streets. The main streets in many Irish towns are not remarkable for their spectacular beauty but Tralee is better than most. In fact, there is an Irish saying that most Irish main streets – the longer they go, the mainer they get.

Tralee's main church of the Holy Cross was designed by Pugin – and looks like it, too.

MacGillycuddy's Reeks and Killarney

MacGillycuddy's Reeks, the finest name for any range of mountains in the history of the world, stand proudly in Kerry, and Carrantouhill, and Mount Brandon, all worth a hike; so, if you've got your pitons and climbing boots, the challenge of a good climb is there as well. As long as you don't expect me to come along with you. I've only to stand on a footstool for the blood to rush helter-skelter to my head. I've embarrassed myself before now, having to be rescued from sheer rockfaces at least six feet off the ground, while I'm rooted to the spot, motionless with fear. However, if you *must* scale life's peaks, because 'they're there', good luck to you. I'll stay here at base camp, and look after the provisions. Before you climb the Kerry Mountains, though, just one small thing: remember these mountain fastnesses are the very ones from whence, it is said, members of the Kerry Football Team are lured, by the promise of raw meat . . . . I knew a 'mountainy' doctor once. He called himself a mountainy doctor on account of the hiking he had to do, to get to some of his patients. Once he went up to look after some old woman, and she was telling him the story of another old fellow in the village, sixty-five years of age, who had married a young girl of twenty-five. My friend, the mountainy doctor said, 'But, what can ever come of that marriage, he's far too old for her.' The old woman looked at him pityingly, and said, 'You can get a terrible sting from a dying bee.'

> How can you buy all the stars in the sky?
> How can you buy two blue Irish eyes?
> How can you purchase a fond lover's sigh?
> How can you buy Killarney?

A few years ago, an American solved the question; he paid a lot of money . . . . I don't think he owns *all* of it; there's bits of it owned by Germans, too. There are a lot of hotels in Killarney and some people think it has been 'spoiled' – over-commercialised – and why wouldn't it? It is one of the most beautiful spots in the world and the locals who haven't a great deal to support them, apart from tourism, can hardly be blamed for trying to exploit and make the best of it.

There are plenty of places for you to stay, if you decide to visit Killarney, plenty of places for you to eat as well, but you really ought to take a sidecar or your own hire car and go up to 'Heaven's Reflex' and drink it all in . . . . There is a beautiful golf course in Killarney, as well; you can take the old 'sticks', and hit a few balls around. After you've picked the twenty-fourth out of the lake, your view of Killarney might be a little less favourable than it was in the beginning; but an even-handed balance can be restored

KILLARNEY

St Mary's Cathedral was built in the 1840s in an 'Early English' style, and was designed by Pugin – again.

THE TARBERT FERRY

The ferry which crosses the Shannon between Tarbert in Co Kerry runs to near Kilrush in Co Clare – handy for golf at Lahinch BELOW.

with a little smoked salmon, a tender Irish steak, a pint of the black stuff, and a ball of malt to chase it all down. If it *is* golf you're after, Kerry, like any other county in Ireland, can provide plenty of it and much of it severe enough to drive you to an early grave – Ballybunion – there's a course there that would put years on you. Rather like Lahinch, it's a course for battling the elements – the wind blowing in off the sea, the cruel rough that catches your ball and hides it and even when you've found it, you need a ten-ton truck to get it out. I spent a holiday as a lad down in Ballybunion with my family. It is a famous place for drinking, Ballybunion; people used to come from all over just to have a drink there, the pubs never closed. I tell a lie. They closed, everyone went out on the street and then the side door opened again, and everyone went back in. Ballybunion had other things to recommend it, the likes of which you wouldn't get in places like Kilkee: Seaweed Baths, where a body could lie and let the iodine do its fine work amongst the pores and corpuscles. Nothing very gracious about it, just a concrete affair, rather like a block house. In you went, took your towel and plunged into the seaweed. It smelled like a Limburger factory and upon exit, so did you. Why is it that anything that's supposed to do you any good at all, either smells or tastes like the Wrath of God?

We stayed in a little boarding house along by the beach and we met there a very nice family from London, who came to Ballybunion every year; they had no Irish connections whatsoever. They were from Leyton, and followed the Orient – I've looked at the Orient's results ever since. The trouble it must have taken them to get down to Ballybunion. By the time they'd taken the train from London to Holyhead, the mail boat from Holyhead to Dublin, the train from Dublin to Limerick and then a bus from Limerick to Ballybunion – half the holiday was over by the time they arrived, but they went every year – they liked the people, they liked the food, they liked the easy going nature of it all. They might even have enjoyed the 'getting there' but speaking as one who has only once taken the mail boat from Holyhead, and marked the occasion by throwing up over his new suede shoes, I find it a little hard to believe.

If the charms of Ballybunion begin to pale, you can always take a ferry across the Shannon to Clare and knock yourself out on Lahinch golf course once again. I took that ferry, once upon a time, with some friends; you can put a couple of cars on it, and it takes about three-quarters of an hour to cross the Shannon, which at that point, is extremely fast flowing and has very strong currents. One of my friends claims to have swum that channel in about half an hour. It was the same friend who claimed that, once upon a time, he killed a shark with his bare hands on the beach at Tralee Bay. Apparently, it had been annoying his sister, so, clasping a sheath knife between his teeth, he dived into the breakers and carved the shark up. He also knocked out the Irish heavyweight, Jack Doyle, with a single blow. And all this, long before Rambo . . . .

THE LANDSCAPE AROUND KILLARNEY AND THE MACGILLYCUDDY'S REEKS

Some of Ireland's most beautiful and unspoiled country lies either side of Killarney: to the west are the MacGillycuddy's Reeks, to the east is the National Park and caught in between are Killarney's three famous lakes. Echoes of that great old crowd-pleaser: 'Oh Ireland! Isn't it grand, your look!"

THE MACGILLYCUDDY'S REEKS

The snow-capped Reeks seen from the Ring of Kerry

The Reeks seen from Killarney's Lower Lake

A little lough between the Reeks and the Purple Mountain

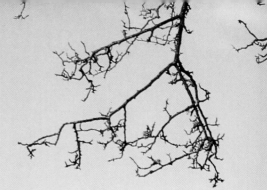

Killarney Lower Lake

Between the Reeks and Killarney

LEFT AND BELOW *The Gap of Dunloe is a wild and beautiful place, and a great gathering place of botanists.*

The Reeks seen from Moll's Gap

THE KILLARNEY NATIONAL PARK

Sunrise and sunset over Lough Leane –
the former looking towards Killarney,
the latter taken from Muckross.

Upper Lake looking towards Torc
Mountains

Lough Leane in the evening, taken from
Aghadoe church

*Muckross Lake looking towards the
Purple Mountain*

Lisdoonvarna and The Burren

Since we appear to be in Clare again, it might pay you to have a look at Lisdoonvarna, another remarkable sociological phenomenon of Irish life where, in the quondam days of my nonage, for two weeks every year the eligible, and indeed, ineligible, bachelors and spinsters from all over Ireland would gather, like swallows over Capistrano. Every single hotel, boarding house, apartment, corregated iron shack and tent was taken. Lisdoonvarna became a throng of single Irishmen and single Irish women, of ages ranging from eighteen to eighty, from spritely young students to decrepit old farmers who had every prospect of coming into a bit of land some day. The matchmakers took over.

There is a story told of a famous matchmaker who recommended a certain lady to an eligible bachelor. When the bachelor had seen her, he said, 'But she's ugly.' And the matchmaker said, 'Ah well, not in the dark.' And the bachelor said, 'But you told me she had two farms, and she's only got one farm.' 'Ah yes,' said the matchmaker, 'but it's a big one.' 'But,' says the fellow, 'she's got a limp.' Replied the matchmaker, 'Only when she walks.'

Many an Irish marriage is made in heaven, but just as many were made in Lisdoonvarna. There was dancing and drinking and love in bloom there. I hope it still goes on, if only for two weeks in the year.

The most remarkable sight in Clare is called The Burren. A limestone plateau, the like of which you will find nowhere else, except perhaps, on the Steppes of Russia. On this limestone plateau all manner of plants, which could scarcely be called indigenous to the area, grow. People come from thousands of miles to look for Edelweiss on The Burren and search for esoteric flora.

THE BURREN

The Burren is one of those places that the Irish have tended to ignore, but increasing interest is now being shown because outsiders are so fascinated by the geological peculiarities. Disappearing lakes and rivers, caves, alpine and arctic flora, terraced limestone pavements . . . this place has the lot. Take the time to drink it all in – and don't tell me you haven't got the time. As we always say: 'When God made time, He made plenty of it. . . .'

Galway

Galway is no more than a brisk stroll from Clare, indeed nowhere in Ireland is more than a brisk stroll from anywhere else, if you have a good pair of walking boots and a stick. You can go up many an interesting boreen and meet many an interesting person. You might also get lost, but you won't get mugged .... You'll find that in Ireland, particularly in the country districts, the towns, the villages, the roads, everybody will have time to talk to you. The Irish are a naturally friendly and gregarious people, they want you to like them, they want you to like their country. And you'd better, as well, if you want to leave the place intact ....

GALWAY

Galway is on the River Corrib and has been in existence ever since a settlement was made near the ford across the river.

The salmon leap in the river
Corrib: from here, thousands of
salmon can be seen as they travel
up-river during the spawning
season. Galway Cathedral ABOVE
was built between 1957 and 1965
in a style which has been called
Classic-Corinthian – I wonder
what on earth Pugin would have
made of that.

CONNEMARA

Connemara is a rather bleak landscape, totally unproductive but very beautiful.

Most of my memories of places in Ireland are inspired by summer holidays in them. It used to be just as much a decision for my father as it is with all of us these days, to know where to take the family every year, but this was long before the Costas Brava, Del Sol, Blanca or Smeralda; you more or less stuck to your own patch when you went on holiday. When I grew up and had to earn my keep, my family actually went to the Isle of Man on one mad, adventurous holiday. They were ahead of their time.

Galway is on the Corrib, a wonderful salmon river and indeed, if you stand on the bridge over the Corrib, you can look down and see the salmon, huge great grey fish, swimming up-river towards the falls. Somehow, you always expect salmon to be pink, like the tins . . . . Galway is the centre of Gaelic Ireland. The West; whence the native Irish were driven by Cromwell and successive plantations. 'To hell or Connaught . . . .'

The province of Connaught includes Galway, Mayo, Leitrim – stony, barren ground, where nothing grows, the grass is too scarce for a cow, and only sheep and goats can

Ben Gorm, on the right, is typical of the stark Connemara mountains.

thrive. They still speak Gaelic in some parts of Galway and Mayo and on the Aran Islands, as they do in the remoter parts of Cork and Kerry.

My holiday in Galway was spent in a boarding house, as always, and near the beach. In common with all the Irish beaches, it's a symphony in fine sand – you don't always get the weather to lie on Irish beaches, but they're marvellous when the sun breaks through. At Galway we caught many a mackerel off the end of the pier – they used to give themselves up. The boarding house we stayed in was appalling – a waitress without any teeth, rooms without hot and cold running water; I don't remember whether, as in the Blackpool tradition, there was 'free use of cruet', but I doubt it. The food was dreadful – that toothless crone I can picture still, sending us out every day with her blessing: 'Out you go now,' she'd say, 'and work up an appetite for your tea.' We'd come back to a little bread and marge. My father actually brought back some mackerel that he'd caught – I don't know who ate them, but we certainly didn't.

My wife's family, on her father's side, come from Galway; their name is Joyce. So popular and so numerous is the name of Joyce, that a whole area of County Galway is referred to as 'Joyce Country'. Galway and Connemara are spectacular in a different

CONNEMARA

The Twelve Bens mountains are rugged and rocky.

*Collapsed cottages are sadly a feature
of the bleak Connemara landscape.*

A wild Connemara pony

CLIFDEN

On a clear day from Clifden, they say you can see the Statue of Liberty . . . . This attractive market town is known as the capital of Connemara. Not far away, on the headland above Mannin Bay, Alcock and Brown landed at the end of their first TransAtlantic flight in 1919.

way to Cork and Kerry. Harsh terrain, rocks everywhere, stone walls, cottages that saw their last inhabitants in the 30s and perhaps even as far back as the Famine. Not many people live there now, waves of emigration after the Famine continued right up to the 50s and 60s in Ireland and now, with the weakness of the Irish economy, thousands of Irish boys and girls – and the youth of Ireland is proportionately greater than any other European country – thousands of them are leaving to settle in America, mostly illegally, or to work in Europe. It is a hard land to make a living on, it always has been. On a clear day from Clifden, you can see the Statue of Liberty, but scenery butters no spuds . . . .

Mayo

Mayo's land is even harsher, many of its sons found employment in Britain after World War II in the 40s, 50s and 60s. Usually it was second and third sons, for the first son was coming into the farm, and that was to be his responsibility. There is a town in Mayo called Bohola – a town of only a couple of hundred inhabitants, but its sons have been so successful that at the last count the number of millionaires in America and Britain that came from Bohola, number about twenty; ten per cent of the population. It wasn't, you see, that they didn't want to work, it wasn't that they hadn't the brains, it was just that there was nothing for them in their native place. In Mayo too is Castlebar; I have been privileged on a number of occasions to compère the Castlebar International Song Contest – you have to hand it to these small little Irish towns, their ambitions are enormous, their inhabitants see no limits and, when people talk of the Irish inferiority complex, I point them in the general direction of Tralee and Castlebar, with its International Song Contest – they've brought singers and songwriters from all over the world for a week of songwriting and singing. I flew into Castlebar with Acker Bilk once, on a little private plane from Dublin airport. We landed on the runway and watched a wall at the end of it rushing towards us; Acker Bilk has never been the same man since. We stopped some ten yards short of the wall – they'll never put a Boeing down there, I can tell you that.

In Mayo, also, is Knock, where at the turn of the century, another religious miracle was seen – a passer-by claimed that he had seen a vision of the Holy Family. Again, the religious enthusiasm and faith of the Irish inspired them to come to Knock in enormous numbers, and indeed, they still do – it is a continuing miracle; perhaps not as big or well known as Lourdes or Fatima, but big enough for the local parish priest, a few years ago, to conceive a great plan. He was going to build a basilica at Knock, just as the French had built at Lourdes and the Portuguese at Fatima. He was going to publicise *his* Virgin Mary, as they had. People would flock in even greater numbers to Knock, to pay tribute, pray and to hope for a miracle. And so, he built his basilica. You may have seen pictures of it – most impressive, indeed you may also have seen pictures of the tap from which Holy Water can be poured to take home and bless yourself with. But the parish priest was not pleased. Yes, hundreds, nay thousands, of people were coming to Knock, but he wanted more. He conceived an even greater plan, an International Airport, where great jets could land and pilgrims would pour in from not only Ireland and Britain but all over the world, from America, Latin America, Europe . . . . The priest persisted, in the face of all opposition, in the face of all common sense, perhaps, but then faith has little to do with common sense. The priest built his runway and his airport and the jets come in providing the cloud cover isn't too low and deposit the pilgrims. He must look down on it in pride, for he passed away a couple of years ago. He left behind him a place of great faith and prayer, but also of cheap knick-knacks and plastic images, as well as a political football that comes into play every time the vexed argument comes up between Church and State.

In Mayo is another famous site of Irish pilgrimage and penance, the Summit of Croagh Patrick – the spot where St Patrick was supposed to have vanquished the snakes of Ireland forever; you'll never see a snake in Ireland, that is, not of the animal variety. Croagh Patrick is no easy climb, and many do it in their bare feet, to pray for themselves and their loved ones. A short step from Mayo and Connaught, is Ulster, Lough Derg and County Donegal where you will find St Patrick's Purgatory, on an island in Lough Derg. It is said St Patrick had a vision that anyone coming in penance there would be forgiven for their sins. It's been a place of pilgrimage and penance for the Irish since, probably, the thirteenth century. People go there to be forgiven their sins, but you'll also find many young couples there, praying perhaps for a happy marriage, or students praying for good exam results. You row out to the island, and do your purgatory as St Patrick did his, in your bare feet – three days and nights of prayer, fasting and abstinence and very little sleep, with only water to quench your thirst, and hot water, with pepper to stave off the pangs of hunger.

On the south side of the harbour is Leenaun (on some maps, this is Leenane), a pretty little village nestling at the foot of the mountains. It is a very popular place with both anglers and climbers.

Ben Gorm is on the north side of the harbour, and seems almost to slide into the sea.

KILLARY HARBOUR

A *Killary Harbour is a long, deep inlet of quite incredible beauty: it is sometimes called Ireland's only fjord.*

B *Westport is a planned town and was designed by the Georgian architect, James Wyatt. The River Carrowbeg is seen here flanked by the Mall and is especially pretty in the summer.*

C *The Atlantic Drive on the way to Achill Head. Achill Head is the westerly tip of Achill Island. Reverting once more to my youth, this was a place where young men and women would go on holiday in the summer. It was a young people's holiday place, and there was a great deal of drinking and roistering and a fair amount of dancing too.*

D *Clare Island in Clew Bay*

E *Clew Bay seen from the Corraun Peninsula to its north*

F *Westport is on Clew Bay which boasts some of the best sea angling in Europe, hence the annual angling festival.*

C

D

F

Knock

In 1879, apparitions of the Virgin Mary were reported here, and Knock is now a place of great pilgrimage – Ireland's answer to Lourdes. The enormous basilica seats some 20,000 people.

Knock has developed into a major commercial enterprise, and cheap plastic images and mementoes abound.

The Calvary Cross and another shrine, 'not-to-be-touched' – one of a series of tableaux which encircle the Cross and depict various stages of the crucifixion.

CROAGH PATRICK

A *On the south side of Clew Bay is the sharp-pointed mountain of Croagh Patrick where St Patrick is said to have fasted for forty days and nights. Shrouded in mist, this photograph was taken from the east of Westport which can be seen in the foreground.*

B *On the last Sunday in July, there is a mass pilgrimage to the summit. Many pilgrims make the ascent in bare feet, running serious risk of cutting themselves not only on the sharp quarzite stones but also on the debris left by the soft-drink sellers.*

C *A small chapel has been built on the summit. Pilgrims themselves transported the building materials to the top – 2510 feet up.*

D *The view from the summit of Croagh Patrick is magnificent. All the little islands in Clew Bay can be seen in this photograph, as can the north coast of the bay.*

LISCANNOR

St Brigid is Ireland's other national saint, and there's even less of her history documented than St Patrick. Many people believe she was an early Celtic goddess who was adopted by the Church for her own purposes. The Holy Well at Liscannor in Co Clare attracts cheap mementoes as at Knock.

LOUGH DERG IN CO DONEGAL

This is another major place of pilgrimage since St Patrick's Purgatory celebrates the saint during the summer months. My wife went here as a young girl: I don't know whether it was to pray for a good husband and if it was, I don't know whether her prayers were answered.

Living at Killiney

When first married, my wife and I bought a little bungalow in Killiney, on the south side of Dublin Bay. The Irish like to think that Killiney Bay rivals Sorrento for its beauty. I've never been to Sorrento but it must be pretty good, if it's anything like Killiney. There's a grand, deserted beach there too, where you can have a bit of a paddle while drinking in the scenic delights of Bray Head to your right, and Dalkey Island, with its little round tower, on your left. If it's even more solitude you're after, you can nip across by boat to the island from Coliemore, the world's smallest harbour. And I forgot to

On Killiney Strand, reminiscing about the good times we had when we lived here. Whilst the beach is a popular one in summer, it can be wonderfully deserted at times.

Looking across Killiney Bay to Bray Head, and the coastline that is said to resemble Sorrento.

<u>KILLINEY</u>

Some of the typically Victorian houses in Killiney.

mention, there are wonderful views across from Killiney Bay to Howth Head on the north side of Dublin Bay. Most of the evenings of the formative years of my youth were spent searching for a party, which, inevitably, in summer took the diaphanous form of a phantom barbecue on Killiney Beach. As soon as the pubs, clubs and bona-fides were closed ('bona-fides' were pubs, shrewdly located outside the city limits, where you could drink until they called the cattle home, owing to a hole the size of a tinker's cart in the bye-laws. They've closed it up now. Many never recovered from the shock) off we'd pop in somebody's old banger, to the phantom barbecue . By the time we'd got there, and stumbled about the beach for a while, the party was long gone. Never so much as a charred chipolata did I ever see. Every so often, above the wind and gusty showers, could be heard some eejit trying to pick out a Bob Dylan song, but of barbecue,

The views from Killiney are spectacular. Dalkey Island can always be distinguished by the little round tower: you can go there by boat from Colliemore harbour, said to be the smallest harbour in the world – but that may be another Irish claim that's not strictly true.

HOWTH

On the north side of Dublin Bay is Howth, originally a Danish settlement. The gardens of the castle are open to the public and remain open until sunset.

birds or booze – nothing . . . . Following the shoreline, by the coast road, will take you through the little town of Dalkey (pronounced 'Dawkey' – and while we're at it, Dundalk is 'Dundawk' – never mind how the BBC pronounce it . . .) to Dun Laoghaire (pronounced 'Done Leery', take my word for it). It used to be called Kingstown, in the great days of Empire, and it's still an imposing place with granite steps, and buildings, dignified yacht-clubs and formal gardens that sweep towards the sea. Dun Laoghaire is an old Victorian port, the scene of much sadness in Ireland over the last couple of centuries. Many a migrant has seen his last sight of Ireland, as the mail boat slipped away from Dun Laoghaire harbour and out across the Irish Sea to Holyhead, a new life, and a new future in Britain; perhaps even further afield. I hope the bands still play on Dun Laoghaire pier on a Sunday – it used to be a favourite Dubliners' pastime, to take the bus or the tram out to Dun Laoghaire, listen to the band, and walk up and down the pier, with its lovely views of the sea, and over there, on the north side of Dublin Bay, Howth Head.

There is the lovely Hill of Howth, far-famed for its train, and Howth itself, a haven of restaurants and folk-singing taverns.

Howth Harbour was designed by Captain Blyth, he of 'Bounty' fame – the man who got thrown off the boat by Fletcher Christian and the boys; I'm not sure whether he designed the harbour before or after that rather nasty hiccup in the history of the British Navy, but when he designed Howth, he made a hash of it, they tell me. You have to be very careful trying to get anything into Howth Harbour when the tide's against

The sun sets over the Bull Wall, the barrage which juts out into Dublin Bay to keep the tide out of the harbour. It is said to have been designed by Captain Bligh and apparently he did a better job on this than at Howth.

Ireland's Eye from the other side, photographed from Portmarnock, another marvellous beach, much loved by generations of Dubliners.

you. I had a nasty accident myself there, once. Occasionally, my father would break the rule of a lifetime, forsake the sea-bass at Baltray, and go with my Uncle Charlie and me to Howth, where we would cast our lines off the pierhead into the sea in the hopes of a mackerel, or a pollock, or e'en a pinkeen. I used to watch the other boys doing it; they simply picked up their weight at the end of the line, and flung it into the sea. I did that for a while, until the hook got caught in the middle finger of my right hand; caught and buried itself pretty damn good. They took me back to a Dublin hospital, where an apprentice-butcher removed the hook as if he'd spent a lifetime at Torquemada's knee. And you ask me why *I'm* not a fisherman?

The Wicklow Hills and Mountains overlook the City of Dublin, and generations of Dubliners have used those hills and mountains, loughs and valleys as a place to escape the city at the weekend for picnics, or just for a Sunday afternoon drive. Glendalough, Roundwood, the Glen of the Downs, Sugar Loaf – an easy climb, from which you can see virtually all the east coast of Ireland, almost to the mountains of Mourne, as you look north, and to the very tip of Wexford, as you look south.

My wife tells of picnics in the Wicklow Mountains with her mother and father and the rest of her family. Her father has always lived in the manner of a minor feudal baron. He

From here, many an Irish-man or woman has seen their last sight of Ireland as they set off across the Irish Sea to Holyhead and perhaps a new life

Just beside James Joyce's tower at Sandycove is what's always been called the Forty-Foot. This is where Dublin gentlemen of every age – including Buck Mulligan from the aforementioned Joyce's tower – would dive stark naked into the chilly depths. It is still a preserve of gentlemen only: the women bathe on the other side.

is the kind of man who insists that before he eats his soup, it be put on the window sill outside the kitchen door – the better to cool. Back rashers are all that meet his favour, and fillet steaks – he feeds well and he likes his comforts. A remarkable man, now ninety years of age and still hale and hearty, still striding the middle of the road with his walking stick, yellow tie and fine Crombie overcoat. In my wife's younger days, he would deign to travel with the family to the Wicklow mountains for a picnic, but with all mod-cons – he had to have his boiled bacon, and cabbage and potatoes, all of them cooked, with extreme difficulty, over a primus stove. He lives now, and bestrides, Tullow

<u>The Mountains of Mourne</u>

Seen here across the lough from Carlingford in Co Louth

in County Carlow. County Carlow is the Midlands of Ireland and generally regarded by Irish people as a little on the quiet side. I've never thought so. In fact, I can hardly hear myself think when I'm there. The place is a cacophony of noise, and the villain of the piece is the country's most prominent inhabitant – the crow, or rook. Ireland, at least in my limited experience, is not rich in bird life, except for the guillemots and gannets, seagulls by the million on the coast, corncrakes and curlews, but more than that and more than anything, rooks, crows – millions of them. As you drive along the road, they congregate before your car, only dispersing, rather like the pigeons in Trafalgar Square, at the last minute, and then if you look out through your rear view mirror, you'll see them settling on the middle of the road again. I've never seen birds congregate on the roads in Britain, but the crow, or rook, obviously thinks Ireland belongs to him.

The Last Words....

And that's about it, the height of it. I promised you no Cook's Tour, just a personal stroll down a sketchy memory lane. It's years since I've been back to see most of the places I've been talking about – if they've changed, I'd rather not know. Anybody who's ever been to Ireland for longer than a wet weekend could write several books on what I've left out, but then, any one of the country's thirty-two counties could keep you going for a lifetime. The best this book can do is whet your appetite, hone your anticipation of your first, or next, visit to Ireland. I hope it keeps fine for you and, sure, even if it doesn't, the rain is soft and the welcome warm.

Go n-eirí an bóthair leat . . . .

Index